Yarns of a Professional Gongoozler

Tales of English Canal Life at Dixie's Marina

by

R J Adams

authorHOUSE®

AuthorHouse™
1663 Liberty Drive, Suite 200
Bloomington, IN 47403
www.authorhouse.com
Phone: 1-800-839-8640

First published by AuthorHouse 5/20/2008

ISBN: 978-1-4343-8220-7 (sc)

Printed in the United States of America
Bloomington, Indiana

This book is printed on acid-free paper.

Gongoozler: An idle and inquisitive person who stands and gazes at the comings and goings of the boats on the canals.

English Dictionary.

Dedicated to all the marina staff, boat-owners, and workers on the inland waterways of England and Wales who, albeit unwittingly, helped to create this book......
and to my wife, Trish, for her never-failing love, support, and patience.

Author's Note

The British canal system stretches over two thousand miles, much of it passing through some of the most attractive and peaceful areas of countryside to be found in England and Wales. Occasional urban sections provide a wealth of historical detail relating to an industrial heritage long passed into the pages of history.

Canal boating and boat ownership is a rapidly developing industry, and inland waterways marinas are continually being constructed throughout the system, to accommodate the steady increase in steel narrowboats and GRP cruisers that now abound.

I entered the business both as a marina manager and narrowboat dweller. During the course of some twelve or so years I met some amazing people, saw some incredible sights, and laughed uproariously at a plethora of amusing incidents.

Each of the eight stories, though self-sufficient, are interlinked and best read consecutively. They are based on my own personal experiences over twelve years as an inland waterway's marina manager. Most of the events described actually occurred, but with the exception of 'Molly", all characters have been fictionalised and bear no relation to anyone, living or dead.

Also available as an eBook or AudioBook from the author's website:
SparrowChat.com

Contents

The Day That Lennox Mannion Got His Own Back

B ack in 1972 when Dixie's Marina was constructed, it was the biggest on Britain's inland waterways. Johnny George Dixon, 'Dixie' to his intimates, had a keen eye for business. While the government of the day hotly debated the viability of maintaining a canal system dating from the early 18th century, and which many politicians considered an expensive white elephant, Dixie foresaw an era of pleasure-boating on the canals that would become a veritable goldmine for those who were 'in' at the beginning.

Financial colleagues scoffed; his bank manager squirmed uncomfortably, but Dixie ignored them all, purchased ten acres of canalside farmland adjacent to Chumpley Lock, and moved in the diggers and bulldozers. Within six months there were jetties placed to moor three hundred boats. Most considered it foolhardy, when figures showed there were less than seven hundred craft licensed to use over two thousand miles of canal system.

Long lengths of waterway were silted and impassable. The deep-hulled working boats that had kept the silt from settling were gone, fallen prey to railway networks more efficient at moving coal, iron ore, and other bulk items in demand for national consumption. The only traffic left, a few enthusiastic pleasure-boaters undeterred by silted shallows and reed-infested locks.

But Dixie knew that where now there were few, others would follow, and one day there would be many. Meanwhile, he helped matters along by lobbying his many friends in high places - a favour here, a touch of blackmail there - until some of those in the halls of political power began to reconsider the worthlessness of those 'stagnant, stinking ditches', and raised less objection when the time eventually came to vote on whether they should stay, or be obliterated forever from the landscape.

Within two years of Dixie's Marina officially opening, half the berths were occupied and more were being filled each month. When I arrived there in 1981, the marina was thriving and Dixie was spending every winter in Florida.

I needed a dwelling, but was short on funds to purchase a house, so decided to live afloat, thus fulfilling a lifelong dream and staying free from the exorbitant mortgage rates of that era. I invested all my savings in an old, fifty-foot narrowboat and went looking for a suitable mooring site. Dixie's was ideal for me; nicely situated amidst quiet countryside, yet close enough to civilization to not feel too isolated.

I was fortunate that Dixie was not in Florida on the day I visited. We got on fine from the beginning and he found me a spare berth, even though the marina was officially full. Not only did he provide me a mooring, but eventually a much needed job selling canal boats and generally looking after the site. Within a couple of years, Dixie decided to retire and spend all his time in Florida. He bestowed on me the grand title of General Manager, and left me to run the place for him.

It was around that time I first met Old Bill. Roy and Betty Blackman had just leased the rundown canalside shop at Dixie's. Most of their lives had been spent in the retail camera trade and they knew best what attracted customers. Before long, the renamed 'Betty's Canal Emporium' had turned into a veritable Aladdin's Cave, and rapidly became popular with passing boaters. Roy and Betty also sold the diesel fuel, and for a fee pumped out the toilet tanks in the narrowboats. Or rather, they employed Old Bill to do it for them.

Old Bill was probably no more than sixty-two years old when he accepted the position Roy jokingly called, 'Fuel and Pump-Out Manager'. He was a dumpy little guy, about five foot two and with a round, cheery face that grew ruddier as the day progressed, partly due to the exertions of the job, but mainly because of the diminishing bottle of Scotch Whisky kept just out of sight under the counter at one end of the shop, where he also kept his cash tin and the numerous pork pies, custard tarts and other confectionaries that disappeared into his ample paunch during the course of a day.

Roy often joked that he never needed a watch. He could tell the time of day by the colour of Old Bill's countenance, or the level of amber liquid in the liquor bottle.

Not that Old Bill could ever be considered alcoholic. His customers were quite unaware of the true reason for his ruddy expression, and Old Bill never slurred his words or missed his footing. He was as cheery and good-natured first thing in the morning as he was at five o'clock in the afternoon, and would go to any lengths to ensure his customers were happy and satisfied.

Unless, that is, the customer was Lennox Mannion.

It was Roy Blackman who first made me aware that Old Bill displayed more distaste than the rest of us for Lennox Mannion. We all agreed Lennox was obnoxious. Even those close to him admitted he was not the most charming of individuals. He'd shot to temporary stardom in an old, long running TV soap-opera from the late-sixties, made pots of money but degenerated into obscurity by the mid-seventies. Excessive living doubled his girth and ruined his liver, but to Lennox Mannion's ego he was still a star to be worshipped and admired by lesser mortals, on whom he would dispense a haughty and conceited indifference. And that included his wife.

To say that I was taken aback when Roy informed me the reason for Old Bill's intense dislike of Lennox, would be an understatement. It never really occurred to me that Old Bill had any *sexual* urges. No one knew his background and we all assumed he was an inveterate bachelor, with no interest in women whatsoever. Consequently, when Roy told me it was affection for Greta Mannion, coupled with the contempt that Lennox showered on his wife, that caused Old Bill's blood to boil each time Lennox hove into view, I was flabbergasted.

Unlike her husband, Greta took pains to preserve a figure once seen dancing on the West End stage. Though in her late-fifties, she was still an attractive woman who resisted the excesses of her husband's lifestyle and accepted his boorish, ill-mannered behaviour with dignity and quiet fortitude.

Thankfully, their lavish, seventy-foot narrowboat was not moored at Dixie's, but further up the canal above Chumpley Lock, which emptied its water into the marina whenever a boat passed through. But ours was the only refuelling and pump-out station on that stretch, so Lennox Mannion and his wife were frequent visitors throughout the boating season. Usually, they locked-down into the marina early on a Saturday to take on fuel before the weekend cruise, which explained why Old Bill dressed casually all week yet appeared resplendent in white shirt and tie every Saturday morning.

It was one particular weekend in mid-summer. A weekend that promised no difference from any other, and probably would not have been, had the cranky old pump that sucks the waste out of a narrowboat's forty gallon toilet tank not chosen that Saturday morning to gasp its last and refuse to suck another drop.

The Mannion's had taken on fuel as usual. Lennox was his normal obnoxious self, finally disappearing below deck to replenish his glass and leave Greta to manoeuvre the big narrowboat out from the quayside and away down the canal. Old Bill watched her go with a far away look in his eyes.

The very next boat alongside required a pump-out, and it was then that the old pump groaned, wheezed, and finally gasped to a standstill in a cloud of smoke and minced sewage.

Now, for those unfamiliar with the sanitary arrangements of an average narrowboat, I'd better explain that onboard toilets are fitted atop a large holding tank from which a wide-bore pipe extends to the deckhead above. Use of the toilet involves opening an airtight valve in the bowl to allow access to the tank; closure after use seals the tank and prevents unwanted odours from entering the boat. Chemical additives help reduce the tank's content to a more fluid state.

When a tank was full, Old Bill connected his pump-out pipe to the boat's deckhead fitting, turned on the pump and sucked out the contents until the tank was empty. Boaters could find it frustrating if their tank was full and there was no way available to pump it out.

Consequently, on this particular Saturday morning, Roy spent four hours glued to his telephone, trying desperately to find a replacement. It had happened at the worst possible time; one of the busiest weekends of the season. Everywhere he rang, he was given the same response. Pumps were available, but not till after the weekend.

It was early in the afternoon when George Anderson, who owned a farm just up the lane, called at 'Betty's' for his weekly pack of cigars. Roy's face lit with relief when George announced he had a suitable pump and was happy to loan it until a new one was procured.

"Mind yer," grinned George, "It's a bit m' powerful than yers, and it's reciprocal…it'll blow as well as suck, so yer'd best be sure the lever's set right!"

George was accurate about his pump. It was much bigger and heavier than the old one. There was much grunting and heaving before finally it was located into place and all the necessary pipework reconnected. It was a powerful beast, with a lever on one side that determined whether it would suck in or blow out. Roy tied it securely with string in the 'SUCK' position, telling Old Bill that he couldn't be too careful with all the kids around the marina. If one of them moved the lever when no-one was looking, it could cause a nasty accident; maybe rupture a toilet tank with the pressure. Old Bill nodded wisely, noting every word.

Soon, the pump-out bay was doing a brisk trade once more. The new pump was much more powerful, and only took half as long to empty each tank. Boaters were in and out again before they knew it, and Roy was grinning from ear to ear as Old Bill's cash tin rapidly filled with money.

For the rest of Saturday and most of Sunday, the pump roared away almost continuously. Come Sunday evening, boats were queuing for the pump-out before returning to their mooring berths, and as the boaters came alongside the quay, all talk was of a rumpus on the Mannion boat that previous night.

The tale was told how Lennox, more drunk than usual, had gone out to dinner with Greta at a restaurant some miles down the canal. After consuming an extremely hot Madras curry, Lennox picked a fight with the manager over some trivial matter. The police were summoned, and the Mannion's eventually expelled from the restaurant. On returning to their boat, Greta had remonstrated with her husband, who responded by blacking her eye with a vicious punch before collapsing into a drunken stupor. The combination of curry and gin fermented inside Lennox overnight, confining him to bed except for frequent, painful excursions to the toilet, and forcing Greta to return the boat next day with no assistance from her husband.

At the time, no-one really noticed that Old Bill was quieter than usual. We were all busy with other customers. It was a warm summer's evening, just the weather to attract the nearby townspeople canalside, whether boaters or not. 'Betty's' was full of customers, Roy was run off his feet, and I was showing a family from Birmingham over boats on the sales row and only vaguely noticed Greta Mannion bring her boat alongside the pump-out quay, though the bruising around her left eye was obvious, even at the distance. Of Lennox, there was no sign.

The family from Birmingham were typical of Sunday afternoon visitors. They had no real interest in purchasing but 'thought it might be nice to look inside one.' I patiently steered them through a neat forty-footer, and was just emerging through the rear cabin door when there was a deep, low 'KER-R-RUMP!' from inside the Mannion's boat. The sound was reminiscent of a dull, underwater explosion, and followed almost at once by a muffled shriek from inside, continuing and growing to a loud, intense wail of anguish.

Making hurried excuses to the family from Birmingham, I ran across to ascertain the cause, just in time to see Lennox Mannion emerge onto the back deck of his boat, covered from head to toe in what can only reasonably be described as an obnoxious, brown mess. He staggered about, eyes rolling, and seemed momentarily unable to grasp his dilemma. Then he saw his wife standing by the tiller arm and began to swear and curse at her as though the whole incident was her fault.

It will never be known if Greta felt she was acting in self-defence, or simply decided enough was enough, but in one swift movement she seized a boathook from the cabin roof and jabbed viciously in the direction of her husband's midriff. Lennox did what anyone else would do when confronted by a sharp, steel-point thrust in their direction; he took a few rapid steps backwards. Unfortunately for him, a narrowboat is aptly named, and though his first two steps connected with the deck, his third left him poised in mid-air above the water, into which he rapidly disappeared with another shriek that trailed off to gurgles.

By the time he finally made it to the bank and kindly strangers assisted him to dry land, the marina frontage was ten deep in gongoozlers trying for a better view, and most were grinning openly at his discomfiture. Lennox stood momentarily, not knowing where to look. Then, with no sound apart from a squelch of waterlogged shoes, he slouched back to his boat and disappeared below, without even a glance at Greta as he passed.

That was the last anyone at Dixie's saw of Lennox Mannion or his wife. Within a week their narrowboat was on the market, and rumours circulated the cleaning company required a full two days to sanitize the bathroom.

We never discovered exactly what occurred. Lennox had obviously awoken from his stupor in urgent need, and not realizing the boat was at the pump-out quay, opened the toilet valve and squatted just as Old Bill connected up his pipe. It seemed inconceivable that the 'Diesel and Pump-Out Manager' had not noticed anyone in the bathroom, given that the deck fitting was near to the toilet window and movement would be visible, even through the frosted glass. But then, it was late in the day and the bottle beneath the counter was close to empty. Old Bill was equally adamant he had no idea who had cut the string and swung the lever of the pump to 'BLOW', instead of 'SUCK'. He just shrugged, insisting that with so many people about, it could really have been anyone.

Eventually, the incident became just another of those boating tales about which people love to reminisce at the end of a hard day's cruise, over another glass of gin. Life at Dixie's Marina went on much as before. Old Bill continued at his job as 'Diesel and Pump-Out Manager', though use of George Anderson's leviathan had been discontinued, pending the arrival of a less powerful machine that sucked in only one direction. All that changed was Old Bill's dress on Saturdays and Sundays. A couple of weeks after the Lennox Mannion incident, Roy noticed at the bottom of his trash can, a rather sad and crumpled necktie, heavily impregnated with what was probably a mixture of pork pie grease and whisky.

It was three years later, almost to the day, when Roy Blackman unlocked the door to 'Betty's Canal Emporium' one Saturday morning to find that Old Bill was not sitting in his usual place on the step, waiting to be let in. Three hours later, he still hadn't arrived for work, and Roy telephoned the police.

They found Old Bill in bed, stiff as a board and cold. No one can drink a bottle of whisky a day and live forever, and it had finally taken its toll of our 'Diesel and Pump-Out Manager'. That Old Bill had died happy could not be contested. They found him with his face set in the broadest possible grin, so much that the funeral people had a job to straighten it out enough to make him look presentable. On his bedside table was the inevitable tumbler of whisky, half consumed, and tightly clutched in one hand a copy of an old and faded magazine, open at an article on a much younger Lennox Mannion, TV star, together with his new bride, Greta.

Old Bill passed, reliving the memory of his greatest triumph; the day he avenged his only love. The day, quite literally, that Lennox Mannion got his own back.

HOT GOSSIP

Had Daphne Forbes-Jackson realized the hassles she was storing up for herself, she would probably never have chosen that particular name for her new narrowboat. It was not as though she was a great fan of Edward Lear. It was more about money really, or more accurately the lack of it. When the builder offered to knock sixty quid off the paint job if she chose a name that included the word 'Owl', she jumped at the idea. It was, he had said, one of his 'Owl class' boats, and as such it merited good advertising for his yard.

Anyway, it could be argued that the problem was not the name so much as the colour; or maybe a combination of both. A bit of a 'chicken and egg' situation really. At first, she had loved the colour. The combination of flaming red cabin sides framed by yellow bands, with a midnight blue roof and bulkheads, had seemed very eye-catching. The little thirty-footer, though not by any stretch of the imagination a 'pretty' boat, certainly attracted admiring glances from the other moorers at Dixie's Marina, in its new, gleaming livery.

Neither did the problem become immediately apparent, due to the little boat initially having no engine and consequently not leaving its marina berth. Daphne had run out of money before the craft was completed and the sleek, twin-cylinder diesel earmarked for under the aft deck had already been transferred to another 'Owl' under construction at the yard. The builder raised cynical eyebrows when Daphne suggested a second-hand petrol outboard be installed under the deck.

"Oh…just for the time being." She had added, hastily, noting manifest disapproval on the builder's features.

With much muttering on the subjects of "death of tradition" and "women boaters" he had set about reshaping the weedhatch to accommodate an elderly, Volvo Penta short-shaft that had been lying around the yard since time immemorial.

Daphne had to admit his work was faultless, though when he finally arrived at the marina in a borrowed van, and sidled along the jetty with hat pulled low, the Volvo Penta tightly wrapped in old sackcloth, his demeanour was more a murderer disposing of a body, than a respected boatbuilder. But then, respected boatbuilders generally don't install elderly outboard motors into their brand new creations.

Not that anyone would have known. The old engine purred away quietly under the deckboard, and though occasionally in hot weather it would gasp for air and die, happily ran again if left for fifteen minutes to catch its breath.

It was all Roger's fault, of course. Had Roger not run off with that floozy from the university and packed in his advertising job to become a mature student, she might have screwed him for alimony and child support. Instead, he had left her and Cassandra almost penniless, unable to pay the rent on the apartment, and with barely enough cash to purchase the tiny boat that was now their full-time home.

Still, Daphne admitted to herself that she was happier than she had been in a long while, and even Cassandra seemed to take life afloat in her stride. "Though…" her mother thought ruefully, "…seven year olds will usually adapt to most things… it may be different when she's a teenager."

Finding Dixie's Marina had proved a stroke of luck; an ideal situation for her. She had worried that a canal bank mooring might be her only option, and finding Dixie's with its huge lagoon, pontoon moorings and lots of facilities, had quite taken her breath away. More so, when they told her that, "Yes, they could find a spare berth for the *"Owl & the Pussycat"*, as it was a relatively small boat.

At weekends the marina was chock-a-block with moorers, and they had welcomed her with open arms. Almost literally, in the case of that bearded guy from the fifty-footer on the next pontoon, who chatted her up for ages until his wife finally screamed at him from across the water, demanding his immediate return with the sarcastic comment that, '…she was *his* wife and he'd better not forget it!' Daphne was glad. She hadn't liked him much anyway. He was too smarmy, and insisted on standing just that bit *too* close to her…

And then there was May and Jack Trumpton, of course. They lived on "*August Moon*". It was difficult to ascertain which of this elderly couple peddled the more perverse gossip. Daphne made the mistake of accepting an invitation to "…drop in for a cup of tea anytime you're passing, dear…" and the resulting stereophonic cacophony of personal, intimate information that had assailed her ears caused a headache for the rest of the day. It seemed May and Jack Trumpton knew everything there was to know about every moorer on the marina, and took malicious pleasure dispersing that knowledge amongst all who cared to listen. She soon realized these innocent-looking senior citizens were purveyors of poison and slander. Daphne deftly avoided their interrogation into her own affairs and eventually escaped with a sigh of relief, determined never to fall into that trap again.

Sunday evening was the time she loved the most. Sunday evening saw them all going home; back to their semi-detached houses and Monday morning blues. They clattered down the pontoons, waved their goodbyes, and staggered to their cars with the vast quantities of goodness-knows-what that they had emptied out of them the previous Friday.

Slowly, tranquillity descended on Dixie's Marina. The last narrowboat was emptied; the last car trundled from the carpark, and as the sun began its long descent from the heavens, the only sound to break the stillness was an occasional 'plop' of big carp breaking surface, or a gentle 'moo' from George Anderson's milkers grazing in the next field.

Daphne perched atop a barstool on the back deck and decided that life had definitely been worse. Cassandra played in her tiny cabin, happily colouring Rupert Bear, the three digestive biscuits begged earlier postponing an eventual demand for more solid evening sustenance. It was high summer and still three hours till dusk. Daphne suddenly felt an urge to take command of her craft and venture forth, if not onto the high seas then at least out onto the 'mainline', as experienced boaters called the stretch of canal that passed not fifty metres from her mooring jetty.

Since the boatbuilder had fitted the Volvo Penta, a week previous, she had only once plucked up the courage to untie the ropes and take the boat out from its berth. Quite late one evening she discovered the water tank empty, compelling a cruise through the moorings to the nearest available faucet. It had been a frightening, though exhilarating experience. She had sailed dinghies in her youth, been junior champion of her local yacht club two years running, but a narrowboat was different; not really a boat at all. More like a ship. By the time they arrived safely back on the mooring jetty, her mouth felt dry and her heart was beating wildly.

Now though, she decided, it was time for a real voyage. Maybe even a lock.

"No," she thought, "I'm not quite ready for a lock, yet!"

But she knew that by turning left under the old railway bridge, the canal stretched lock-free for almost a mile. Part way down, past Farmer Anderson's fields, was a sheltered, tree-lined haven, almost opposite a winding hole used for turning the bigger narrowboats, and a favourite mooring spot for boaters seeking seclusion from the clamour of the marina. At this time on a Sunday, it would probably be deserted.

"We'll go there, tie up, and I can cook supper."

Her heart gave an extra thump at the very audacity of the thought, and knowing that if she waited too long her nerve would give out, she quickly removed the bar stool from the deck, lifted the deckboard and squeezed the rubber bulb in the fuel line that served to prime the outboard. She envied boaters who just pressed a button, or turned a key, to start their engines. The old Volvo Penta hailed from times pre-electric-start, and the wooden deckboard needed precarious balancing on her left shoulder, so she could lean into the engine well and yank the recoil rope that would spin the machinery into life. Fortunately, the motor fired second pull and she emerged from under the board in a cloud of blue exhaust smoke.

A tousled, blonde head appeared in the cabin doorway. Cassandra questioned the sudden vibration, but on being informed of the pending adventure, shrugged her shoulders disinterestedly and returned to Rupert Bear. Her mother deftly released the mooring ropes, blipping the throttle as the "*Owl & the Pussycat*" moved sedately into the mainline.

Safely negotiating the old railway bridge, Daphne settled back to enjoy this rural canal stretching as straight as an arrow into the distance. The evening was idyllic; larks twittered in the firmament, and the only indication of human intervention was a boat approaching way in the distance.

Despite disappointment over the loss of her diesel engine, she found herself warming to the old outboard motor under the stern deck. It was so very quiet, not at all like the vibrating, thudding monsters she had heard on the marina, belching clouds of sooty smoke and causing anything not lashed down, to rattle incessantly.

The farmer's fields lay well astern, the winding hole just fifty yards ahead, when the other boat's arrival required a manoeuvre toward the right bank, to allow clearance for its passing. *'Marston Brook Hireboats'* was painted on the side in big, red letters. Two adults and a small child, a girl much younger than Cassandra, occupied the stern deck. The man waved, the child leapt up and down excitedly, and pointed, "Look, Mummy, it's the *'Owl & the Pussycat'*!" The scream of delight, short-lived, transformed to a pout, hands thrust onto tiny hips, "…but, it's the wrong colour! Why isn't it pea-green? It's supposed to be pea-green, Mummy!"

Daphne thought the flood of tears, rapidly developed into a full-blown tantrum, was overdone even by the standards of a six year old. The woman looked daggers at her, as though she were to blame for the child's outburst. Fortunately, the two boats separated quickly, but an echo of the infant's howls still wafted faintly on the breeze as Daphne moored her craft to the old wharf by the winding hole, stopped the engine and went below.

Cassandra, bored with painting Rupert Bear, the door to her cabin and part of the wardrobe, had begun pulling the stuffing from an old rag doll. She required to know why the little girl had been so upset. Daphne explained about the colour difference, while vigorously scrubbing the boat clean of her own daughter's graffiti, forging a mental note never to buy her oil paints. Cassandra declared the girl extremely silly, and demanded food.

Her mother set a small folding table in a wooded clearing adjacent to the old wharf. It proved a delightful place to have supper, and long after Cassandra had become bored with the scenery and returned to dismembering her rag doll, Daphne lingered, drinking in the tranquillity and another cup of coffee.

The thud of a big diesel disturbed her reverie as from behind the tree-line another hire-boat hove into view, a solitary male figure at the tiller. Daphne noted with approval how he slowed the engine as he passed her boat, so as not to make a wash, then as he reached to open the throttle again, he paused, looked across at her and shouted, "You know, that boat's the *wrong* colour!"

The fixed smile stuck; glued to her face long after man and boat were gone.

The sun had drifted into the treetops and wind rustled leafy branches far above. It was almost twilight in the woodland glade as she packed away the supper things and folded the little wooden table. From the stern deck, looking up towards the marina, she noticed that it was still quite light out in the open, away from the trees; the old railway bridge was blurred, but just visible in the distance. She went below to check Cassandra had washed behind her ears, but the little girl was on her bunk fast asleep, rag doll innards strewn all over the floor. Her ears would have to last the night, washed or unwashed. Daphne strongly suspected the latter.

"At least the fresh air and active lifestyle wear her out," she thought, sinking onto the bunk that also served as a settee, "No problems with insomnia, or pining for Roger."

Not that she expected much pining. Roger had been fairly un-noticing, even for an unofficial step-father. He was hardly ever home, and on the rare occasions he deigned attendance, showed little interest in the child, or her activities.

"Or mine, for that matter," Daphne muttered to herself.

She couldn't decide whether to curse Roger, or thank him. His Liverpool apartment had been pleasant enough, but she hated city life. It would be nice to live in a Welsh cottage again, like the old, ivy-clad dream-home she and Cassandra's father had briefly shared when they first married.

A court had cleared the driver of any blame, when on that dark, wet afternoon in January her husband had absent-mindedly stepped into the path of the moving bus. He had always intended to take out life insurance once Cassandra was born, but the accident occurred three months before that event, and put paid to any chance of Daphne remaining in their home. Three years alone with a baby, in the tenement council flat provided for them by Social Security, blurred her judgment just enough to accept Roger's offer and move into his apartment with him. It was two years later when she discovered the term 'his apartment' really meant, 'the landlord's'.

Daphne brushed away a tear, angrily recalling her thirtieth birthday. He'd finally returned home just after eleven at night and she'd given vent to hysteria even before the bombshell burst. Staying just long enough to pack some clothes, he calmly informed her he was moving out and into the arms of another woman. Once he had gone, and the urge to trash his things had been overcome without succumbing to temptation, she sat up most of the night, contemplating her future. There was the small legacy from her parent's will. Roger knew nothing of that. The high interest account recommended by the local bank manager had failed to increase its value substantially; not enough to keep the apartment going. She would take Cassandra and leap off the Mersey ferry before returning to a tenement council flat……but it was then the idea had hit her. Surely, it would be enough to buy a small canal boat; to live on the water.

"And all the rest is history," she thought, glancing out the window, then leaping to her feet as she realized it was almost ten o'clock and pitch dark outside.

There was no moon and for a while she fumbled about on the back deck trying to get her bearings. Fortunately, her eyes accustomed quickly to the gloom and she was able to make out a silver ribbon of water stretching ahead into the distance, though the old railway bridge that marked the entrance to the marina was lost in the darkness.

Daphne turned off all the interior lights, except for a nightlight in Cassandra's cabin. The Volvo Penta was incapable of charging the boat's two batteries, and the big tunnel light on the foredeck would need lots of power if she was to stand any chance of negotiating the old railway bridge without hitting anything. Though quite dark, enough light reflected from the water for her to navigate safely till she reached it, and hopefully there would be no other boats about at that hour of the night.

A stiff breeze tugged at her hair once the boat left the shelter of the trees, and little wavelets slapped and gurgled against the hull. It was really very pleasant boating in the darkness and Daphne relaxed against the stern rail, guiding her craft through the water with a light touch on the tiller bar.

Long before she reached it, the old railway bridge stood out, silhouetted against a warm glow from the marina lights beyond, but as she drew closer glare began to affect her night vision and she crossed her fingers that no other boats were moving about. It was pitch black on her side of the bridge and no-one, however vigilant, would see the "*Owl & the Pussycat*" approaching.

Daphne determined to leave the tunnel light until the last possible moment. If the batteries failed before she had navigated the bridge, the boat would hit the side for sure. She closed the throttle, slowed to a crawl, until less than a boat's length away from the structure. Then, as darkness was about to engulf them utterly, she flipped the switch. The tunnel light blazed out, illuminating everything, including the two people on the towpath under the bridge, who stood rooted and unbelieving.

The woman had her back to the wall and the man was facing her. His trousers sagged limply around his ankles and the light reflected off a pair of pink buttocks protruding from beneath his tee-shirt.

Daphne, stunned by this unexpected scene, opened the throttle wide and roared under the bridge, plunging everything behind her once more into darkness. She pushed the tiller bar hard over, swung the boat around towards the mooring jetty, crunched the engine into reverse, and more by luck than skill, backed neatly into her berth. It only took a few moments to secure the mooring ropes, connect the dockside electrics that charged the batteries, silence the engine, and then she was below in the welcoming warmth of the cabin, the door slammed shut behind her.

Over a hot cup of tea, she pondered on the risqué tableau so briefly unfurled before her eyes. Daphne had immediately recognized the bearded guy who'd chatted her up so insistently during her first weekend at the marina. She laughed out loud, recalling his shocked features bathed by fifty thousand candle power. The woman had cowed down behind him, hiding her face from view, but Daphne was sure of one thing, it quite definitely was not his wife. The female who had leaned out of their narrowboat's front doors and harangued him for flirting, bore no resemblance to the woman desperately grabbing at her underwear out on the towpath.

"Oh, well," she thought, preparing for bed, "it really isn't any of my business."

24

Next morning the marina was quiet, as always on a Monday. Ken, the groundsman, trundled up and down astride his ride-on mower, waving as Daphne sipped her morning coffee on the back deck. A wisp of blue smoke idled casually from the chimney stack of "*August Moon*" and the occasional car scrunched the gravel of the parking area as visitors arrived or departed. Of the bearded guy and his illicit amour, there was no sign. His boat seemed deserted, as he had left it the previous afternoon when Daphne watched him drive out of the marina with his wife.

"He must have taken her home and come straight back with his fancy woman," she thought, "I wonder what excuse he gave to get away with that?"

Any further speculation halted abruptly as Cassandra, face like thunder, appeared in the doorway with a towel and toilet bag hanging from her arm. Stubborn insistence that she really had no need to shower that day as she'd not done the slightest thing in any way to make her dirty, cut no ice with Daphne who shooed her to the showerblock with a stern warning not to lose the key.

Dismissing all thought of the bearded guy from her mind, she focused instead on the previous afternoon and the sheer pleasure of cruising down the canal to have supper. She determined they would do the same thing that very evening.

Sure enough, by seven o'clock the "*Owl & the Pussycat*" was once more slipping from its mooring and down towards the old wharf. The weather, perfect yet again, remained so all week, and by Friday her evening voyages had become almost routine, though she made a point of returning to the berth each night before dusk.

This idyllic time in her life was marred only by a constant reference to the colour of her unfortunate craft, almost every time another boat went past. Most thought their remarks witty, but some were downright rude. As the weekend approached, these constant, shouted remarks stretched Daphne's nerves to breaking point. She could think of no response to the perpetual barrage. It *was* the wrong colour, but she could hardly scream down the canal that, 'Yes, it was called the "*Owl & the Pussycat*", but it definitely was *not* the pea-green boat in which Lear's unlikely couple went to sea!'

To aggravate matters, Cassandra was going through another of her trying phases. Only yesterday she had stuffed a small teddy bear down the boat's toilet. It had fallen through into the holding tank and Daphne, wrinkling her nose with disgust, had to plunge an arm into the smelly effluent to retrieve it. That very morning before breakfast, when Daphne had scolded her for playing near the end of the jetty, the child had swung round in a tantrum, accidentally striking her mother's head with the boathook she had been using as a fishing pole.

Now, Saturday breakfast was over. Daphne banged the coffee mug down on the cabin roof. Her head ached from Cassandra's swipe, and she turned reluctantly towards the cabin doorway to begin her daily chores. It was then she noticed him stood behind her on the jetty. His first words sent a flush of anger coursing through her veins.

"You shouldn't be boating at night, you know. The Water Board'll prosecute you."

The eyes held an aloof arrogance, accentuated by a slight curl of his upper lip. She noted that the point of his beard waggled up and down when he spoke.

"Oh, really," her reply drenched in sarcasm, "and you're the expert? What you were doing was perfectly legal, I suppose?"

"I don't know what you mean," he sneered, "I was simply taking an evening stroll with a friend."

"Oh? And just how far can you stroll with your trousers round your ankles?"

The question struck home. The bearded guy's face flushed with rage.

"Now look!" He took a step towards her, wagging a finger right in her face, "I don't want my wife hearing any false rumours about me...understand?"

Daphne smiled, and said with sweet acidity, "I wouldn't dream of spreading any *false* rumours about you, rest assured."

"Good." The bearded guy relaxed, withdrew his finger. He stepped back, deliberately eyeing her up and down, from head to toe. "You know," he continued eventually, "You're really a very sexy babe. Why don't we have dinner sometime? Perhaps I could teach you some more...rules of the canal...?"

This brazen, lascivious suggestion was too much for Daphne. She fought the urge to punch him in the mouth, swallowed the bile rising in her throat, and gasped, "Get lost, you creep! I wouldn't have dinner, or anything else with you, if you were the last man alive. You're repulsive!" She turned away and started through the doorway into the cabin.

The bearded guy shrugged, "That's your loss. Let me know when you change your mind." He began to walk away down the pontoon, then stopped and turned around. Her back was to him but she heard him say, "Oh, by the way…you do know that boat's the wrong colour, don't you?"

The echo of his laughter followed her down into the cabin.

Fifteen minutes later, Daphne Forbes-Jackson stepped off the "*Owl & the Pussycat*" and walked purposefully down the pontoon and onto the path that led around the marina. She eventually arrived at the narrowboat called, "*August Moon*", and leaning over the back deck, rapped loudly on the cabin door. The grey-haired old lady seemed pleased to see her.

"Why, hello dear!" she exclaimed, "Come on in. The kettle's just boiled. Would you like a cup of tea?"

Daphne smiled sweetly. "Thank you, May," she said, stepping briskly down into the narrowboat's interior, "I'd really love one. Oh, by the way, you'll never guess what I saw the other night…though you must promise *never* to tell a soul…"

THE LOSS OF THE 'YORKSHIRE LASS'.

George Bettisfield's foray into canal boating was relatively short-lived, and everyone at Dixie's Marina breathed a sigh of relief when it was over. To suggest that George was a strange man would be an understatement. I heard many comments on his character, and by far the most endearing was that, '…he maybe had a difficult childhood'.

We all recognized he must have some redeeming features, but despite much screwing-up of faces and prolonged head scratching, no-one could come up with any.

Afterwards, there was the usual post mortem gossip around the marina and everybody agreed that, putting aside a person's character, it is a fact of life that handling a narrowboat requires expertise, and some folks just never seem able to learn.

Whether any were as calamitous as George Bettisfield, is still hotly debated.

Narrowboats are not easy craft to handle. In any but the balmiest of conditions, they seem more inclined to go sideways than in the direction their skipper's intend. It's the flat bottom, of course. Flat bottoms create less resistance in the water than, say, a keelboat, and although Olympic swimmers may insist that a flat bottom is a definite asset, what aids an Olympic swimmer can be a downright liability with a narrowboat. Of course, the reason for a flat bottom is simply that most canals are ridiculously shallow, and any other form of hull-shape would gouge into the silt, effectively preventing sideways drift, but hardly enhancing forward motion.

All of this is compounded by a canal often less than thirty-five feet wide, and an average narrowboat length of fifty feet or more. Given the phenomenon of sideways drift, it is perfectly feasible in theory, and occasionally in practice, to travel the canal with one's bow scraping the far bank from a farmer's field, while the stern end methodically demolishes the incredibly expensive carbon fibre fishing poles of the local angling club, who just happen to be holding their annual 'fur and feather' on the towpath side.

With a little practice, most owners quickly develop an innate ability to counteract their boat's alarming habits, though all but the most egotistical would admit that even those with impeccable expertise can fail on the odd occasion. It's all part of the great charm and excitement that attracts hundreds of new boaters onto the canals each year, many hiring fifty and sixty foot monsters for their first experience afloat. That the canals are not strewn with wrecks and blocked by grounded boats is testament to the average person's ability to adjust quickly to the foibles of such steel leviathans.

Of course, there is an exception to every rule, and at Dixie's Marina that autumn it was George Bettisfield.

I had known George's father, Joe Bettisfield, for a number of years. The old man kept a fifty-footer at Dixie's, an old but tidy narrowboat called '*Yorkshire Lass*'. He used it frequently during the season, travelling down from his native North Riding to spend two or three weeks at a time on the boat. Then age and ill-health caught up with Joe and the '*Yorkshire Lass*' sat forlornly at her mooring for months with no sign of the old man, until a letter arrived from his solicitor telling us Joe had passed on, and asking for a breakdown of the mooring invoice.

I only realised he had a son, following a chance remark one afternoon when I helped Joe berth his boat in a particularly vicious squall, and commented that he could do with a good crew. The old man, pausing only momentarily to gauge the wind strength, spat expertly into the lagoon and complained his son and only living relative was, "n'but a us'less li'bil'ty wi' borts o' anythin' el'". Other, barely interpretable mutterings basically translated to George being an arrogant, pig-headed, lout who thought he was good at everything and in fact "… wer' gud fer not'in'". They had not spoken for two decades, and the old man stated categorically that he was not about to begin now.

Whatever the shortcomings of the late Joe Bettisfield, events testified to him being an excellent judge of character.

After Joe's death, we all expected '*Yorkshire Lass*' to be sold as quickly as possible, so it was with some measure of amazement that I beheld a beetroot-faced, thick-set, and rather belligerent individual in a camel-hair coat, enter my office one early October afternoon, announce he was George Bettisfield, and demand his father's boat keys. Even then, we all assumed he was just looking over the boat, prior to sale. On his return, he marched brusquely into my office without knocking, and gruffly demanded details of the mooring charges. When informed all fees were paid till the following March, and it was the policy of the marina not to make refunds, he rudely accused me of swindling his dead father out of five months mooring money, finally stating if that were the case he would make use of the 'old steel hulk' until next March, then decide what to do with it.

The weekend following George Bettisfield's visit was 'officially' the last of the season. After a summer best remembered for gale force winds and lashing rain, this weekend produced warm sunshine and balmy airs; a temptress to those boaters already contemplating next year's holiday on Spain's Costa del Sol. Many owners had already surrendered to the weather and sheeted-up their charges for the winter, but enough were about to still cause a queue at Chumpley Lock on this particular Saturday morning. The lock forms an entrance to the marina, as the main canal passes by the side of the lagoon and out under the old railway bridge at the far end. Consequently, all boats turning right out of Dixie's have to pass through Chumpley Lock, which causes boaters some inconvenience on a Bank

Holiday weekend in high summer, when the queue will often stretch half a mile passed the old railway bridge, but is not normally a problem in mid-October.

It was around one-thirty in the afternoon when my gaze, idly drifting from a sales brochure on the office desk, noted four boats on the towpath side of the canal waiting to lock up from the marina. Had there been five, the ensuing two minutes might have proved disastrous. A puff of blue diesel smoke drew my attention to a narrowboat moving rapidly out from the lagoon in the direction of the towpath bank. At first, it seemed likely the throttle had stuck open, for the boat careered into the bank at full speed, narrowly missed the last boat in the line, and came to rest against the towpath, pointing towards the old railway bridge. It only took a moment to identify the narrowboat, "*Yorkshire Lass*", and even from the distance I had no trouble recognizing the beetroot countenance of George Bettisfield at the helm. The thin, tight-lipped, ascetic woman seated on the foredeck, arms folded and ignoring his gesticulations, I assumed to be his wife.

At this point, events had not yet steered me to the conclusion that George Bettisfield may be one of those rare individuals who should never be allowed to set foot aboard any type of floating craft, though I have to admit my earlier dealings with the man aroused curiosity sufficient for me to leave the office and stroll casually up above the lock, ostensibly to stretch my legs. In between chatting to boat owners working the paddles, I noted that '*Yorkshire Lass*' had managed to turn around and was pointing in the right direction. The boat

George Bettisfield had narrowly avoided was entering the lock chamber below me.

"The guy's a bloody maniac!" the man at the helm shouted up to no-one in particular, "Shouldn't be allowed near a boat! Thinks he knows it all, and knows nothin'!"

I recalled old Joe's comments on his son's opinion of his own abilities.

As the lock filled, and the narrowboat rose up to meet us, the boater continued regaling those in earshot with an account of the Yorkshireman's inadequacies as a helmsman. Apparently, during my walk to the lock, George Bettisfield had managed to turn his boat around, demolishing one of the marina jetties and upending a canoeist in the process. He boorishly refused assistance from others boaters, and threatened with the sharp end of a boathook anyone who "lair s'much's a finger" on his craft.

My informant was still muttering on '…the bloody awful people yer come across on the cut these days…', as he and his boat disappeared up the canal.

I anticipated George Bettisfield or his wife would appear at the lock, windlass in hand, to operate the paddles and release the water so '*Yorkshire Lass*' could enter. No boats waited to descend, and I had no windlass with me to empty the lock, so I leaned against the gate-beam, enjoyed the late autumn sunshine and casually surveyed the marina laid out below me, waiting to observe what would happen next.

'*Yorkshire Lass*' was still against the towpath, though I noted its crew had not bothered to secure the boat to the mooring rings provided. George Bettisfield, seated on a high metal helmsman's seat welded to the stern deckboards, gazed haughtily about him like Neptune risen from the depths. His wife sat in the same position she had occupied from the start; on the foredeck, arms folded, mouth clenched shut. From their demeanour, it was apparent they both expected others to work the lock for them.

A large hireboat cruised up behind *'Yorkshire Lass',* spilling teenagers over the towpath. No sooner were they ashore than the youngsters raced up the steep, stone steps to the top of the lock and began ratcheting the paddles enthusiastically. Water poured through the sluices in a mini-tidal wave that rushed down the canal, threatening to send the unsecured *'Yorkshire Lass'* careering backwards into the hireboat. George Bettisfield reacted by thrusting the throttle lever to its maximum. *'Yorkshire Lass',* her old Lister engine belching fumes, began a battle with the current while her skipper sat rigid and unmoving as his boat slowly gained momentum over the decreasing flow, and slid inexorably towards the still-closed lock gates.

Chumpley Lock is relatively easy to enter. Though one of the many narrow locks on the inland waterways, and just wide enough for one boat, the canal funnels gently inwards towards the gates and a narrowboat has nowhere else to go but into the chamber.

It did not matter that George Bettisfield never moved his tiller from the centreline; that he seemed a man in the grip of seizure, right arm rigidly clamped on full throttle. *'Yorkshire*

Lass' knew her way into the lock and steamed down the middle of the canal straight for the still-closed gates.

What may have transpired had the eager, young hire-boaters not managed to open the gates in time, is mere conjecture. As the water in the lock dropped to the level of the canal, the gates swung free and wide, moments before the narrowboat's bows reached them.

Had George Bettisfield closed the throttle at this point, his craft would have floated sedately into the chamber and come gently to rest against the massive, reinforced-concrete sill at the far end, designed to withstand anything that heavy-handed boaters hurl against it, including fifteen tons of narrowboat.

Unfortunately, he remained frozen to the throttle handle, one arm clasped around the tiller, eyes locked fixedly on the concrete sill advancing rapidly towards him. From my vantage point above, I caught a fleeting glimpse of Mrs Bettisfield, still tight-lipped on the foredeck, though her arms were now unfolded, her fingers clutching desperately for any firm support, her eyes bulging more than usual. But then, she was near fifty feet closer than her husband, to the approaching concrete sill.

When a fifteen ton narrowboat travelling at full speed collides with an immoveable object like a lock sill, two things happen. Firstly, the boat decelerates from four miles an hour to zero in a nanosecond. Secondly, the enormous amount of inertial power created by its forward momentum has to go somewhere, and is rapidly transferred to any object onboard not securely fastened down. Such objects accelerate from zero to four miles an hour in a similar nanosecond, producing loud and continuous crashing, rattling and shattering noises from inside the boat.

This was exactly what happened to the contents of *'Yorkshire Lass'*. In a cacophony of destruction, suitcases, pots and pans, TV, crockery, cameras and numerous other items, speedily traversed the length of the cabin, forming a mountain of devastation against the front bulkhead doors. Mrs Bettisfield, herself not exempt from the laws of physics, rapidly slid from her seat and down onto the front deckboards, legs flailing at thin air. Any sound she may have uttered was drowned by the pandemonium within.

George Bettisfield managed to remain in place on the helmsman's seat, anchored by his rigid throttle arm. The violent collision aroused him sufficient to throttle back and ease the bellowing Lister of its load. Otherwise he sat unmoved, staring straight ahead as though nothing were amiss, ignoring the plight of his hapless wife, the damage down below; beetroot-faced and detached, seemingly oblivious of those around him.

The teenagers, enthusiasm unabated by this fiasco, filled the lock and opened the top gate, allowing *'Yorkshire Lass'* to pass on her way.

Without so much as a nod of appreciation to those who worked the lock for him, George Bettisfield once more thrust the throttle to maximum. I watched him continue his erratic journey up the canal, glance off two moored boats and scatter a family of swans, before finally disappearing into the distance.

It was late in the afternoon when stories of a madman loose on the canal began to filter back to the marina. Boaters out for the day returned with tales of near collisions, splintered lock gates, and frayed nerves after encountering the narrowboat, *'Yorkshire Lass'*.

The rest of the weekend passed without further incident. By Sunday evening, George Bettisfield and his boat still had not returned to the berth. Further gossip concerning *'Yorkshire Lass'* and her skipper was subdued, eventually overtaken by more immediate concerns, as moorers prepared to leave the marina and head back to their homes.

The good weather continued over the next few days, but boaters were few and the marina so quiet, that by midweek I determined to have a day away on my own boat, if only for a change of scenery. Consequently, that Wednesday morning saw me up through Chumpley Lock bright and early, determined to enjoy the autumn sunshine, still warm despite a freshening westerly breeze.

The canal was mostly deserted. Once clear of the lock, I filled a mug with steaming coffee from my Thermos and relaxed, determined to enjoy a peaceful cruise. George Bettisfield and *'Yorkshire Lass'* were far from my mind. A couple of miles up the canal, I eased the throttle to pass a Water Board boat and noticed men at work, repairing a damaged section of embankment.

I recognized the gang. "What's amiss, Jack?" I called to the foreman, "Did someone have an accident?"

"Aye…" was the response, "…'appened Sat'day. Some bloody idiot rammed the bank at full speed. Don't know who it was. Farmer saw it 'appen, but didn't recognize the boat and weren't close enough to catch the number. More's the pity!"

I had a pretty good idea of the culprit, but kept my counsel and left the men to their toil. Further on, the Water Board owned moorings, and a dozen or so private boats were tied alongside the bank. I slowed once more to pass them by, and noticed three steel narrowboats badly scraped along the hullsides and a fibreglass cruiser lying sunk on the canal bottom, a huge hole in its offside. Surely this couldn't all be the work of George Bettisfield, could it?

By lunchtime I had reached my selected mooring spot, Calveston Junction, where the main canal is joined by a short arm of just a few miles, leading to some villages in the hills. It's a pleasant section of waterway, attractive to boaters for picturesque views and the quaint old hamlets through which it lazily meanders. I had no intention of traversing the four locks leading onto it, however, and moored below the junction, on the far side of a wide rural basin, across from the stone quay where narrowboats would wait to ascend the lock system.

After a hearty lunch, I settled into a chair on the foredeck with a good book and a freshly opened bottle of Chardonnay. Occasionally, a boat would pass behind me down the main canal and the odd, intrepid hire-boater would negotiate the Calveston flight, sending a rush of water down through the basin to disturb my reverie, until all was calmed once more.

By three o'clock the wind had freshened considerably, and although still sunny, I went inside to fetch a pullover.

It was then I heard the unmistakable thud of a Lister SR3 diesel engine at full throttle, and even before the boat hove into sight I was fairly sure it must be *'Yorkshire Lass'*. That late in the season, it was unlikely any other madman would be churning down the canal at full throttle. I watched from the cabin window as the narrowboat careered into the basin at maximum speed. Fortunately, *'Yorkshire Lass'* was travelling away from my boat and towards the mooring bollards on the stone quay opposite. George Bettisfield, easily recognizable at the tiller, killed the throttle moments before the narrowboat struck the stonework, helped alongside by a brisk wind gusting across the basin.

I stared with dismay at the elderly narrowboat. She was barely recognizable as the trim, orderly craft once owned by old Joe. Dents and gouges blemished her hull, deep scratches lacerated her cabin panels, and I could see at least two cracked windows on the starboard side. Mrs Bettisfield stepped ashore and walked stiffly up towards the first lock, windlass in hand. They obviously intended venturing onto the flight, and up the canal arm.

Calveston Basin is all of seventy-five metres across. The lock entrance is situated midway between two great sandstone buttresses that rise up either side of the gates, gradually losing height as they join the stone quays on either side. Unlike Chumpley Lock, which even George Bettisfield could not miss, the first of Calveston flight requires some degree of steering ability, even on a calm day, if a boat is to negotiate the entrance successfully.

With the wind at her beam, *'Yorkshire Lass'* stubbornly refused to leave the quayside, and scraped tortuously backwards and forwards along the stonework each time George Bettisfield selected 'full ahead' or 'full astern'. Try as he might, no amount of throttle would tempt the narrowboat from the bank, until eventually he signalled wildly for his wife, who had meanwhile managed to empty the lock and open the gates, to return and assist him.

I watched this unfolding spectacle with some disgust and little sympathy for the ruddy-faced, arrogant ingrate who was methodically vandalizing a nice boat. George Bettisfield remained glued to his high metal seat on the sterndeck of *'Yorkshire Lass'* throughout, apparently indisposed to shift himself sufficient to even throw a fender overboard and stop his boat from scraping on the stonework. Though normally happy to help out a fellow boater, I had no intention of offering unsolicited assistance to this insufferable character, so I settled back into my foredeck vantage point and awaited developments with interest.

After much bellowing at his wife, whose ineffectual attempts to push the boat sideways against a twelve knot breeze served only to raise her husband's blood pressure further, George Bettisfield once more slammed the throttle into full reverse. The complaining *'Yorkshire Lass'* ground her way backwards along the quay, towards the main canal that flowed across the basin behind them. With the tiller hard over, and much thrusting of the throttle control, George Bettisfield eventually managed to swing his boat back into the main canal and head to wind. Then, with roaring engine, the narrowboat swung gradually round into the middle of the basin and towards the open lock gates.

Theoretically, in fairness to the man, it was not a bad manoeuvre and on a calmer day may even have proved successful. Unfortunately, the wind was now gusting ever stronger across the basin, and though her skipper seemed blissfully unaware of it, *'Yorkshire Lass'* was drifting sideways almost as fast as she was moving forward. The straight line between boat and lock rapidly traversed to a diagonal, and as the narrowboat's bow approached the lock chamber she became virtually broadside to the entrance, still on full throttle and a collision course with the sandstone buttress.

The resultant crash was quieter than the Chumpley Lock experience. I guessed there was less left inside to break. George Bettisfield, undeterred by the sudden jarring crunch, battled doggedly with his charge, now gripped by the wind and slewing round once more towards the main canal.

In all good faith, I cannot recall the exact number of times this madman drove his boat into the stonework. A saner person would have given up after two, or maybe three failed attempts, admitted defeat and chosen a less hazardous route, or perhaps sold the boat and taken up gardening.

George Bettisfield was not a man to quit.

After a while, the roaring Lister and jarring thuds grew faintly annoying. I returned to my book, only glancing up when another deafening crash disturbed my concentration. He must have been at it for an hour when, following one more bone-rattling thud, the boat swung round, stern on to the lock. Whatever prompted George Bettisfield will never be known, but with a sudden jerk he threw the engine into reverse. Slowly, *'Yorkshire Lass'* inched her way astern, the wind died momentarily, and by a sheer fluke of luck the narrowboat rattled her way into the lock chamber – backwards.

Mrs Bettisfield, patiently waiting on the lockside throughout, swung the gates closed with a thud, obscuring further view like theatre curtains descending on the final act of some comic opera.

It was obvious, however, that this performance was far from over. Curiosity, a desire to know what happens next, prompted me from my chair, into my boots, and up to the top of the lock.

I reached the lockside just as the chamber was almost filled. Mrs Bettisfield was preparing to open the upper gate. Her husband, still firmly rooted to his chair, ignored my approach, glancing occasionally behind him at his wife's activities.

"You do realize the next winding hole is at Abbotston?" I said. Abbotston was a hamlet some two miles distant, and the nearest winding hole to turn a fifty-footer.

After pointing this out, I suggested they lock back down into the basin.

At the proposal, George Bettisfield's ruddy countenance took on an even deeper shade. I noticed some of the muscles in his face began to twitch and took a step back, anticipating violence. Then he spun around to face me, raised his arm and stabbed a finger fiercely towards my chest.

"Wa' asked yer ter interfere?" he shouted, "I know wha' I'm adoin'…s' mind yer business!"

I shrugged. "Suit yourself," I said, and left them to it.

The sun was dipping as I returned to my boat. I loosed the mooring ropes, fired up the engine, and edged out into the main canal for my return trip to the marina. Behind me I heard the rush of sluicegates, and guessed the Bettisfield's had heeded my words and emptied the lock again. Sure enough, within a few minutes the old Lister was roaring at full bore, as the narrowboat emerged from the chamber and churned across the basin. She only came into view thirty or so feet from the main canal bank, and I realized yet again that George Bettisfield had no control. *'Yorkshire Lass'* hit the concrete with a mighty crash. The boat stopped, appeared to shudder, then pick itself up and float casually backwards, like a punch-drunk boxer demanding the fight continue long after the count is over.

I was quarter of a mile ahead before George Bettisfield managed to straighten his charge and follow me down the main canal, but even from the distance I knew there was something amiss with *'Yorkshire Lass'*. It was hard to put a finger on, difficult to pin down, but something in the way the boat rode the water told me it would never reach the marina.

Not that George Bettisfield noticed anything wrong. With throttle wide he drove his craft fast towards mine, but I slowed my engine and allowed him to come closer. *'Yorkshire Lass'* was suddenly three inches lower in the canal, and in a matter of moments it was all over. The Lister coughed once and died; water flooded the exhaust ports. Mrs Bettisfield still sat on the foredeck, tight-lipped, arms folded, as *'Yorkshire Lass'* slowed, settled on the bottom, and the canal rose up around her waist. George Bettisfield remained perched, beetroot-faced, in his metal chair, canal water slopping around his knees. She was a good boat that had taken one blow too many. Welded seams, weakened by stress, had finally parted and she sank into four feet of water.

I turned away, increased speed, until a bend in the canal hid the unfortunate scene from view. It went against the grain to not assist a boater in distress, but I knew that *'Yorkshire Lass'* was beyond my help, and somehow it seemed fair justice to leave her crazed, belligerent crew to their fate.

I never saw George Bettisfield or his wife again. According to the 'towpath telegraph', some passing hire-boaters took them ashore and rang for a taxi. By the time I returned to the marina that evening, their car was no longer in the car park and we assumed they had driven back to Yorkshire.

The Water Board salvaged *'Yorkshire Lass'* next day, with one of their big floating cranes. The final bankside collision had split a weld just aft of the bow section, but that was soon repaired, and Monkton's yard at Granville did the refit.

Had George Bettisfield sold *'Yorkshire Lass'* immediately his father died, she would probably have fetched him twenty thousand pounds, in round figures. Taking into account the salvage charge, claims for damages, repairs and refit expenses, he'll be lucky to break even now. It seems a high price to pay for a few days holiday, and a lot of false pride.

But then, as those round here often say, some folks just never seem able to learn.

THE DEVIL AND 'SARATOGA ROSE'

It was six months after Commodore James J. Trotter arrived at Dixie's Marina, when whispers on the grapevine began hinting that matters may not be as they appeared aboard his boat, 'Saratoga Rose'.

Tales of flickering candles late at night on an old thirty-two foot, centre-cockpit canal cruiser with dodgy electrics, were not in themselves reason for anxiety, though the cramped cabins of the fibreglass boat, coupled with the Commodore's advanced age, may have raised some safety concerns. It was not until Angelina McIntyre burst into my office one Saturday morning, with a white toy poodle under one arm and a large black Bible clutched to her ample bosom, that I began to sit up and take notice.

Angelina was a rather overpowering woman at best, not a real nuisance most of the time, but sufficiently highly-strung to make life difficult on the odd occasion things did not go her way. She was middle-aged, stout, and a rather hysterical lady who owned *'Dawn Adventure'*, a fibreglass cruiser moored on the next jetty to *'Saratoga Rose'*. On my imaginary list, comprising moorers I hoped one day might move on and bother some other marina manager, she was probably near to the bottom, though very definitely, listed. She was loud-mouthed and strident, wore far too much make-up, and hideous red lipstick that earned her the nickname 'Cruella', after the Disney character, by certain younger male members of the marina staff, who had been heard to comment that she was the last person they would want any adventure with, least of all a 'dawn adventure'.

This particular morning, Angelina was in full flow, and had apparently found religion. She began by demanding a move to another mooring, stating she would not remain one more minute near that 'black magician and devil raiser' on the floating den of iniquity next to her. It was only thanks to the presence of the Lord, and the very book she clasped in her hands, that she had not been whisked away to suffer some fate worse than death, by the evil forces invoked the previous night aboard her neighbour's boat.

I calculated the evil force required to whisk Angelina anywhere to be at least on par with an F-4 tornado, but finally calming the lady to a point where I might make some sense of her ranting, and stifling the smirk rising to my lips, I began piecing together the happenings of the preceding evening.

Angelina had arrived at her boat just after dark, alone except for the poodle. She prepared for bed, then, lifting a hand to draw the curtains, noticed a flickering light inside the fore-cabin of *'Saratoga Rose'*. This did not in itself cause particular alarm, until she noticed the silhouette of a naked man gyrating and cavorting in an unholy fashion behind the closed curtains.

Eventually, the light was extinguished and all went quiet, until she awoke in the early hours to discover the poodle had moved off her bedcovers and was whining under the bunk. Hearing a strange 'evil chanting' from outside, she peered through the window and saw *'Saratoga Rose'* bathed in a bright, eerie light. Strange movements came from within. A cloaked silhouette danced grotesquely behind opaque curtains. Her blood ran cold as she heard the evil chanting grow louder. Then, from the forward cabin, Commodore James J. Trotter emerged into the open cockpit, wreathed in a thick cloud of white smoke, clad in a black cloak, and carrying a cauldron filled with burning incense. He quickly set the container down on the cockpit floor and danced manically around before flinging the contents, 'in an evil, ritual gesture' over the side and into the water.

Terrified out of her wits, Angelina remained rooted to her bed, gripped by a fearful anticipation that any moment Old Nick, himself, would appear and carry her off to eternal damnation, or worse.

The Commodore returned to the fore-cabin with his now empty cauldron, and within a few moments all went dark until he again emerged into the cockpit, locking the door behind him, and then proceeded to the aft cabin where, she said, he remained in darkness for the rest of the night.

Angelina, too petrified for further sleep, spent the remaining hours till dawn gripping the Bible to her bosom and reciting the Lord's Prayer, only gaining respite of a few hours rest once day had dawned and the Devil was safely back in his sarcophagus.

At this juncture, I decided it was pointless to differentiate between the habits of devils and vampires. Angelina was not of a mind to take note of such disparity, so I simply agreed to change her mooring for an available berth that was far distant from '*Saratoga Rose*', and she finally swept from my office, muttering on the outrage of such widespread devil-worship and black magic throughout the canal system.

Left alone, I pondered on whether to take further action. My policy was always minimal interference with moorers, but neighbour disturbance was definitely on the list of cardinal sins, and if anything murky was afoot, then it was best nipped in the bud.

The Commodore was a reclusive character. He had lived on '*Saratoga Rose*' for a number of years and when he first applied for a mooring at Dixie's, had seemed a typical ex-naval type; pleasant, forthright, and quite definitely not the kind of character associated with the 'Black Arts', though I was not completely sure how one identified the archetypical black magician. If that were his trade, then he was certainly a very old magician, well into his eighties, though fit enough to dance manically inside a cramped fore-cabin, if Angelina was to be believed.

It was just at this moment Charlie Martin rammed his forty-footer through the jetty on 'J6'. The resultant tirade from adjacent boat owners took so long to resolve, that Commodore James J. Trotter's antics were pushed from my mind until later that afternoon, when on returning to the office, I was accosted by one of my least favourite moorers.

"I've just been talking to Angelina McIntyre. She tells me there's evil business afoot on this marina."

Roderick Mainwaring pronounced his surname 'Mannering'. I've always been highly suspicious of those who spell simple names in a complicated manner. He wore a beard, thinly disguising numerous character defects, and owned a narrowboat moored near the top of the lagoon, by the old railway bridge, and close to Angelina's new mooring. He was one of a small clique of boat owners on that pontoon, who had been at Dixie's for a few years and assumed they had shares in the place.

According to marina gossip, Roderick Mainwaring was recently caught out under the old railway bridge late one night, in a less than flattering position, with a lady who was not his wife. In fact, since his spouse had chased him all round the marina with a boathook just a few weekends back, the subject was still hot on the tongues of those who love to chatter about others' misfortunes.

Although not normally counting myself within that category, on this occasion the rare opportunity to bask in the delight of Roderick Mainwaring's comeuppance was not to be missed, and I had taken no steps whatever to quash the idle gossip. Now, it seemed likely that the man who apprehended me was looking for a scapegoat to draw the heat from him.

"Something has to be done about it," he challenged. "Some of the moorers have been talking, and we've decided he should be run off the marina, as soon as possible."

"Just a minute," I said, incensed by this high-handed attitude, "If anyone takes matters into their own hands, it will be they who are run off the marina…by me! Understand?"

Roderick Mainwaring was not known for courageous resolve in the face of adversity. He raised his hands in a gesture of compliance, "Oh, don't misunderstand me," he fawned, "I wouldn't deem to tell you your job. I just thought I'd warn you that some of the moorers are in an ugly mood, that's all."

"Well, you can tell them that the matter's being investigated, and to keep their noses out of marina business," I snarled, thinking, "If I kept a shortlist of moorers to move on, this guy would be right at the top!"

Back in my office, I contemplated how best to proceed. Usually, in a squabble between neighbours, moving one to another berth resolved the problem, though sometimes they would make up the following week and want to move back again. But this was different and could turn ugly. I decided to pay the Commodore a visit.

It was late in the day before work-pressures eased and freed me to stroll up the moorings. *'Saratoga Rose'* looked deserted as I knocked on the fore-cabin door, but almost immediately it opened and a balding, grey head appeared. The Commodore was on board.

"Come in, dear boy, come in!" he cried affably, "You'll have to excuse the mess though."

I squeezed down into the confined cabin and my nose immediately wrinkled at a slightly acrid smell in the air. I noticed charring on one cupboard, and a small burnt hole in the carpet.

"You must forgive the state of things," the Commodore reiterated, "I'm afraid I may have disturbed some of your moorers last night. Have there been complaints?"

"Well…" I began.

"Old age can be a bit of a handicap, my boy, especially on a small boat," he continued, "and last night while I was taking a shower, one of my candles fell onto the carpet… there." He pointed to the scorched floor covering, "I came out the bathroom to find it smouldering, and without stopping to think, jumped on top to put it out. Of course," he chuckled, "silly old fool that I am, I forgot I had nothing on my feet. You should have seen me dance about…and yell! It jolly well hurt!"

"I imagine it did," I said, feeling relief at such a mundane explanation for at least part of Angelina's story, though I was still not totally convinced, "Did you have any other problems last night?"

The old man grimaced, "That was just the start of it, I'm afraid." He reached over, and with rheumy fingers pulled a tape cassette from its holder on a shelf above the table. "I keep rather late hours, you know…at my age I find I need very little sleep, so after watching television for a while I thought it best to conserve the batteries…television uses such a lot of power, even my little black and white TV…so I began listening to this tape of Gregorian chants…I'm rather partial to such music… by the Benedictine monks of St Michael, you know…?"

I nodded authoritatively, though I'd never heard of them.

"…and, damn me if I didn't fall asleep in the chair, and when I woke…and it's a good job I did…blow me, if another candle hadn't set light to my newspaper…" he motioned to a low shelf at one side of his chair, containing a half burnt candle, "…the newspaper was on the arm, and at some point I suppose it must have fallen down …I probably nudged it in my dozing, silly old fool that I am…"

Peering over the arm of the Commodore's chair, scorching was visible on the woodwork around the shelf. "You'll have to be more careful," I exclaimed, horrified by the old man's narrative, "you could've been burnt to death."

The Commodore nodded, "I know, it was careless of me, but I've learnt my lesson. It won't happen again."

"But, tell me," I needed more information, "What happened when you awoke and saw the newspaper burning?"

He jumped up and dragged a heavy object from behind the chair. "Sand bucket!" he cried, "Old navy tradition; never without one!"

The object was a black, metal bucket filled to within a few inches of the rim with fresh sand. He saw my puzzled expression.

"In case of fire," he explained, "just throw the sand on it. It smothers the flames, you know. Only I'm afraid that last night, being half asleep, I missed my aim and most of the sand landed on my chair. So I grabbed the burning paper, stuffed it in the empty bucket, then carried it up into the cockpit…only, by the time I got there the paper was burning quite fiercely, and the handle got rather hot…burning my fingers…" he trailed off lamely.

"And, let me guess," I grinned, "You dropped the bucket on the floor, danced around clutching your fingers, then threw the burning paper overboard…?"

"With an old rag wrapped round the handle!" The old man beamed, as though we had both solved a major puzzle, "Well, well, my boy, you really are most astute!"

"So much for the forces of darkness," I thought, but kept it to myself.

There was only one other facet of Angelina McIntyre's story that still remained unexplained.

After further admonishing the Commodore regarding fire hazards on his boat, I made a mental note to ask the marina mechanic about an old battery charger that had been lying unused around the workshop for months and which, properly connected to the quayside hook-up, would dispense with the Commodore's need for candles altogether. Then, as I was leaving, I turned to the old man and asked if he had noticed whether the moon was up during his nocturnal activities, the previous night.

"Oh, goodness me, yes!" he enthused, "It was full…you couldn't miss it. Why it bathed the whole marina like a great floodlight. Wonderful sight!"

I thanked the old man and returned down the pontoon, cursing Angelina McIntyre's over-vivid imagination. En route back to the office, I called in at Betty's Canal Emporium for a packet of biscuits. Roy Blackman, the proprietor, grinned when he saw me.

"Sorry," he said, "I don't keep books on witchcraft. You could try the chandlery!"

My snarl was fairly benevolent; Roy and I got on well.

Moorers tended to gather in 'Bettys' to exchange information and gossip, so Roy was a mine of information on matters seething beneath the surface, which often failed to reach my office. He told me how Commodore James J. Trotter had become the latest to top the charts of moorers' gossip that day, knocking Roderick Mainwaring down to second place. Apparently, half the marina were convinced the aged seaman was Old Nick personified, and most of the other half were prepared to admit that he could be in league with the anti-Christ.

Roy chuckled when I told him Angelina's version of the previous night, compared to what had actually transpired on *'Saratoga Rose'*.

He informed me Angelina had entered the shop last evening and asked to purchase a Bible. Whilst not the most obvious item for a marina store, Roy was too keen a businessman not to keep some less popular lines in the stockroom, though he admitted to me the Book required a good dusting, prior to sale.

Delicate interrogation on his part had revealed that a certain young clergyman, waylaid by Angelina at a local cocktail party, had agreed to join her on *'Dawn Adventure'* for a day on the canal, and the lady needed to do some theological revision, prior to his arrival. The bottle of gin, purchased along with the Good Book, was no doubt an aid to memory.

Angelina, soused in booze, and woken suddenly from a drunken stupor with her head still full of the Old Testament, more lucidly explained her interpretation of an old man's innocent antics while endeavouring to prevent his boat becoming a bonfire.

Roy agreed to intercede with the moorers in defusing the situation, and I had the delicate task of informing Angelina that her neighbour's midnight antics were perfectly innocent. On my way back up the marina towards her boat, I was surprised to see a young clergyman in some disarray, rush hurriedly down the pontoon, leap into his car and race out of the marina in a cloud of dust.

Angelina seemed much dishevelled when I boarded *'Dawn Adventure'*. She was not in the best of moods and refused to accept any explanation for the previous night's events, other than her own. I escaped as soon as I could, gave a great sigh of relief once I was back in the shelter of my office, and hoped fervently I had brought an end to the matter.

It seemed that I had.

In the weeks that followed, nothing further transpired to fuel the gossip about Commodore James J. Trotter, and the matter was virtually forgotten. The old man seemed pleased when I presented him with the surplus battery charger from the workshop, and promised in future to go easy on the candles. Angelina McIntyre was now far enough away from her tormentor for her experiences to fade, though she developed a haughty petulance towards Roy Blackman when he refused her a refund on the Bible.

Roderick Mainwaring and his wife left in their narrowboat for a three week summer cruise, and Dixie's Marina reverted to its more normal late-summer tranquillity.

Then quite suddenly, Commodore James J. Trotter suffered a serious heart attack and was rushed to the local hospital, where he died without recovering consciousness. It was a distressing time for the marina staff, who generally got on well with the old man, and having had more to do with him than most, I felt the pain of loss acutely.

There was no family, no living relatives, and so it was the old man's solicitor who eventually gave authority to sell *'Saratoga Rose'*. I went on board to remove the old man's personal effects and fetch the boat onto the sales row.

It was just as I'd seen it the last time I was on board, the day after Angelina McIntyre's fateful night. I placed all his belongings in a plastic bag; clothes, shoes, various artefacts. It didn't seem much for eighty odd years of life.

I tried starting the engine, but the batteries were discharged. They were located under the floor in the centre cockpit. I leaned down, lifted the boards and felt about for the wires. My hands closed on a large, wooden box, and then a round, steel container. The box prevented me from reaching the batteries, so I lifted it into the cockpit, and as I did so the lid fell off. Inside, neatly folded on top, was a black garment. I took it out, unfolded it, and saw a robe with various strange insignia sewn into the fabric. Underneath was a cardboard container of black candles and an old tattered book in a language that I recognized as Latin. Beneath these were a collection of various incenses, a silver pentangle on a neck-chain, and a small bottle filled with a thick, dark liquid.

Reaching once more under the floor, it took both my hands and all my strength, to drag out the heavy, metal, cauldron.

VIKING SHANDY

When Barbara and Stephen first suggested the idea, Daphne Forbes-Jackson dismissed it out of hand. After all, she was only just starting to get the hang of locks. She had only done four, and the last of those had been a bit scary, to say the least. No, it was too silly to consider. Besides, it took three days cruising and umpteen locks just to reach Wolverhampton, and then there were another twenty-one of the beastly things even before one started up the Wyrley and Essington Canal…no, it was too silly for consideration, by far.

It all came about because Barbara and Stephen lived on a seventy-foot narrowboat moored at the top of the Cannock arm, an offshoot of the Wyrley and Essington Canal, and suggested she might like to boat over sometime and visit them. But it would mean, a round trip of nine or ten days, and that was hardly 'boating over', now was it?

It may have been feasible if the *'Owl & the Pussycat'* had been equipped with a proper diesel engine, but to go all that way with only an eight horsepower Volvo Penta petrol outboard under the sterndeck was quite ridiculous. No, it was just too silly by far.

Mind, life had got a bit dodgy at Dixie's Marina since she'd told May and Jack Trumpton off *'August Moon'* about that bearded guy on the next pontoon; the married one she had seen at it with another woman under the old railway bridge. The Trumpton's had blabbed the story to all and sundry. The bearded guy had been giving her some very nasty looks since that day, two weeks back, when just after his wife took tea on *'August Moon'*, she had pursued him around the marina, jabbing at his backside with a boathook.

Daphne admitted to herself that she had told May Trumpton the tale because she wanted it blabbed around the marina, but that was just after the bearded guy got right up her nose with his arrogant sexist remarks, and anyway, she hadn't realized how effective it would be. Perhaps vacating the marina for a week or two might be a wise move. Besides, Cassandra was becoming bored. There were still three weeks before school opened again, and a seven year old on a thirty foot boat with nothing to do…...

Finally, Daphne decided she would set off next day and just see how things went. She would make no plans, take each day as it came, and see how far she got. Then she thought, "Why wait till tomorrow? Why not go now?" With a tingle of excitement, she realized there really was no reason to delay departure. It was early afternoon, with still six or more hours of daylight. Pausing only to inform the marina staff of her plans, and ask them to hold her mail, she loosed the mooring ropes and headed for the entrance to Chumpley Lock.

Three days later, after an idyllic cruise, and with the scratches and scrapes from numerous locks covering her hullsides, the *'Owl & the Pussycat'* berthed at Autherley Junction, where two canals meet and the entrance to a long flight of locks known as the 'Wolverhampton Twenty-One' was a mere fifteen minutes cruise away.

The engine was running low on fuel, and Daphne knew she needed to find a petrol station, and also a supermarket to stock up on provisions. She untied the little folding trolley from its place on the cabin roof, and after loading it with three empty fuel cans, called down into the cabin for Cassandra to accompany her.

The child had hardly left the boat during the voyage from the marina. She rarely appeared on deck, and seemed quite content to view the passing scenery from her cabin window. Daphne wondered how she could stick being down below. The weather had been very warm and the little cabin was stifling. Cassandra seemed impervious to the temperature and played happily with her dolls.

Now, she pulled a face at the mention of shopping, but Daphne's offer of ice cream spurred her from the boat and down the quayside, clasped tightly to her mother's arm.

The shopping centre was a mile from the canal. Cassandra became fractious in the hot sun, and Daphne breathed a sigh of relief when she realised the supermarket also boasted a petrol station. By the time they had bagged the shopping and filled the fuel cans, the sun was lower in the sky, and the air sufficiently cool to make the return journey bearable, even dragging the loaded trolley, and with frequent stops to wipe melted ice cream from Cassandra's face and clothes.

As the *'Owl & the Pussycat'* came into view, they noticed a yellow and green narrowboat called *'Mjolnir'*, moored ahead of them. The cabin side bore a strange hammer-shaped symbol painted above the name, and a pleasant looking man in shorts and long, bushy sideburns lazily rubbed the boat with a wet cloth. Daphne guessed he was probably in his mid-sixties.

As they began unloading the trolley, the man sauntered over. "Hello," he said, with a Manchester accent, "My name's Hundi Mostrarskegg. I'm a Viking."

"Really!" Daphne was taken aback. The man looked quite sane, even intelligent. "You don't sound like a Viking?"

Cassandra poked her head out of the cabin door, "Why's your boat got such a funny name?" she asked, bluntly, "And what's that thing on the side?"

Hundi Mostrarskegg smiled, "The thing on the side is Thor's hammer," he explained, and as Cassandra's brow furrowed, continued quickly, "Thor is the Viking God of Thunder, and he strikes his hammer on rock to create the thunder. In Viking language, Thor's hammer is called *'Mjolnir'*, and that's the name of my boat."

"Um-joll-near," Cassandra repeated very slowly.

"Ye...e...s," said the man, "Well, that's...um, jolly near!"

Hundi Mostrarskegg and Daphne both laughed at this play on words, but Cassandra scowled and went below.

"I suppose you've had to clarify that many times?" Daphne said, "Not many people would know what it was."

"Oh," the man grinned, "I'm sure you've explained just as frequently, why your boat's the wrong colour."

Daphne looked at her red and blue boat and smiled at his perspicacity, "Yes," she said, "It gets irritating after a while, doesn't it?"

Hundi Mostrarskegg nodded, knowingly.

"I don't think you're really a Viking at all," Daphne laughed, "Why the name?"

The man looked solemn, "Oh, dear, you've seen through me," he said, "You're right, my real name's George Bakewell. My wife and I are from Manchester and we're both completely potty on Viking history. I built *'Mjolnir'* in my front garden, and now that we've retired we spend all summer on her, pretending we're Vikings. A bit silly, really…" he ended sheepishly.

"I think it's wonderful!" Daphne cried, "Does your wife have a Viking name?"

"Ondott Bjorndöttir, otherwise known as Helen," he grinned, "She's onboard, if you would like to meet her."

Ondott Bjorndöttir otherwise known as Helen, was a short, rather plump, motherly lady with an agreeable smile and sticky hands. "How lovely to meet you," she exclaimed, dabbing at an oven cloth, "I'm just making lefsa, that's Viking bread. We're getting rather low, and George likes a piece each evening with his supper wine. Would you like to have some?"

Cassandra insisted on trying a piece, but Daphne was not sure, though when she learned it was a form of Nordic potato bread, lightly fried and buttered, she relented and found it delicious.

Hundi Mostrarskegg otherwise known as George, insisted she take a glass of home-brewed damson wine to wash it down, and a tumbler of lemonade for Cassandra, before taking them on a guided tour of the forty foot narrowboat. The interior was beautifully laid out, with Viking artefacts decorating every surface. She was surprised when Hundi Mostrarskegg otherwise known as George, informed her he had built the craft out of fibreglass, not the usual steel plate of most narrowboats.

"It was my job before I retired," he explained, "designing and building reinforced plastic tanks for industry. A narrowboat is basically only a tank with a pointed end."

It was a lovely boat, and Daphne told them so. Then, when Ondott Bjorndöttir otherwise known as Helen, asked where they were headed, she explained her plan to ascend the 'Wolverhampton Twenty-One' and maybe cruise the Wyrley and Essington Canal till they reached the Cannock Arm and a rendezvous with her friends.

"Only I'm a bit nervous of the Wyrley and Essington," she said, "I've heard some dreadful stories; how the kids throw stones from the bridges, and the canal is full of rubbish…so I'm not sure if it's a good idea. We may just stay in Wolverhampton Basin for a few days, and then return."

Hundi Mostrarskegg otherwise known as George, thought for a moment, "I've heard it's better lately," he said. "We were up there about three years since, and then it was quite bad and we had to turn back, but the Water Board's done a lot of dredging recently, and I think a few more boats get up there now, so things have probably improved. It's quite a nice canal in places, though it does wind around some rather insalubrious areas on its way to Cannock." He thought some more, "I'll tell you what," he continued, "we're not going up the Wyrley and Essington, but we're tackling the 'Wolverhampton Twenty-One' in the morning. If you like, we can go up together. Our two boats are just the right length to fit into a lock, and it'll ease the burden no end."

Daphne thought it was a wonderful idea. She had dreaded tackling the forthcoming flight of twenty-one locks on her own. It would be much easier with two boats. The Vikings suggested an early start, before the sun got too hot, so it was agreed they would meet up at the bottom of the flight at seven-thirty sharp.

The next morning dawned bright, with the promise of another hot, sunny day. By seven-thirty, *'Owl & the Pussycat'* and *'Mjolnir'* were both waiting at the foot of the 'Wolverhampton Twenty-One'. The first lock was in a wooded, rural setting and Daphne thought it looked beautiful in the early morning sunshine, not at all what she had expected. Hundi Mostrarskegg otherwise known as George, suggested the *'Owl & the Pussycat'* enter first, so Daphne carefully steered the little thirty footer into the narrow lock, until its bow fender bumped gently on the sill at the far end. Then, *'Mjolnir'* followed them in. It was a tight squeeze and the bigger boat's bow was right up against the *'Owl & the Pussycat's'* stern fender before it was possible to close the bottom gates and open the paddles to flood the lock.

Cassandra was under strict instructions not to venture on deck without permission, but she was quite content down in the cabin playing with her dolls, despite the bumping and scraping as the two boats jostled for position, rising slowly upwards as the lock chamber filled with water.

They negotiated the second lock and were waiting for it to fill, when Hundi Mostrarskegg otherwise known as George, looked back at his boat and said, "Oh, good, it's time for the first refreshments."

Double doors, in the cabinside of *'Mjolnir'* next to the engine room, were open wide, and three tumblers of liquid sat on the gunwhale. Ondott Bjorndöttir otherwise known as Helen, stuck her head out and called, "Come and get it!" She handed Daphne a brimming glass, and said, "We call it Viking Shandy…it's half lemonade and half mead. Just the job when working locks!"

Daphne took a sip, "It tastes wonderful!" she cried, "Do you make the mead yourself?"

"The mead *and* the lemonade," replied Ondott Bjorndöttir otherwise known as Helen, "We have about twenty demijohns of various wines brewing here in the engine room, and there are seven or eight maturing in a special cold compartment that George made, under the foredeck."

Daphne was impressed. "Is it an old Viking drink?"

"The mead certainly is," she laughed, "though I know of no evidence they drank lemonade. Our word, 'honeymoon', comes from the revelous marriage celebrations of the Vikings, who'd drink and dance for a full month following a wedding. It was thought that drinking mead was responsible for fertility and the birth of sons, so newly-weds drank it assiduously for a month, or one 'moon', to ensure their firstborn was male. Woe betides the host that didn't have sufficient supplies to last the full cycle of the moon! Mead is made from honey, of course, and that's where the word comes from."

"That's amazing!" Daphne exclaimed, "It's incredible what one learns on the canal."

And so it was, all the way to the top of the 'Wolverhampton Twenty-One'. Every second lock, Ondott Bjorndöttir otherwise known as Helen, would appear in the doorway of *'Mjolnir's'* engine room with three more brimming tumblers of Viking Shandy, and Daphne would learn a little more of the fascinating history of the Nordic peoples.

By eleven-thirty, they were through the last lock of the flight and moored in Wolverhampton Basin. The Vikings moored up behind the *'Owl & the Pussycat'*. They were continuing along the mainline canal to Birmingham, but the junction with the Wyrley and Essington was only a short way ahead. Whatever her decision, Daphne knew she would have to say goodbye to her new friends, and continue the journey alone.

There was a knock on the cabin roof, and the two Vikings appeared in the doorway. "We're just about to take on the Birmingham mainline," said Hundi Mostrarskegg otherwise known as George, "so we've called to wish you well and say our goodbyes."

Ondott **Bjorndöttir** otherwise known as Helen, held out two bottles of mead and a large flagon of homemade lemonade, "To keep your spirits up if the natives get hostile," she said, smiling. Daphne and Cassandra kissed them goodbye, then waved as *'Mjolnir'* cruised past and out of the basin.

During the ascent of the twenty-one locks, the rural scenery had rapidly transposed to more urban surroundings. Wolverhampton Basin was in the centre of the busy town, and as Daphne watched *'Mjolnir'* and her Viking friends disappear into the distance, she felt suddenly isolated, despite the bustle of traffic around her. The town's ring-road passed over the canal not a hundred yards away. The sounds of buses, motor-lorries and cars pervaded the environment, and yet she felt like a visitor to some alien planet.

"The peace and tranquillity of the canals makes all this seem like bedlam," she thought, with a shake of her head.

Back inside the boat's little cabin, Daphne felt more at home. Cassandra demanded food, so lunch was prepared, and sandwiches made for eating later in the day. "After all," Daphne thought, "who knows when we may next be able to stop."

The *'Owl & the Pussycat'* was about to enter uncharted waters. According to Daphne's canal guidebook, the Wyrley and Essington seemed innocuous enough, but it twisted and turned through many of the poorer areas of the Midlands, before eventually reaching Pelsall Common and the more rural miles up the Cannock Arm to Norton Canes Dock, where Barbara and Stephen's boat, *'Strawberry Fields'*, was moored.

Daphne was thankful there were no locks to worry about. The section of canal they would be cruising was near on sixteen miles, and additional locks may have made the trip too long to accomplish in daylight, necessitating an overnight stay in areas it was maybe best not to moor. Even with no delays, the *'Owl & the Pussycat'* would need six or more hours to cruise the distance. The guidebook showed a Water Board yard at Sneyd Junction, roughly halfway along the journey. It might be possible to moor there safely for the night, in an emergency, but Daphne really preferred to complete the trip before dark, if possible.

To further complicate matters, the little Volvo Penta engine would soon need more petrol. There was nowhere to refuel in the Basin, but Hundi Mostrarskegg otherwise known as George, had mentioned a petrol station near the canal at Wednesfield, just a few miles up the Wyrley and Essington, so it would be necessary to moor-up there.

Realizing she had taken the decision to press on without really being aware of it, Daphne jumped to her feet, "Time to set off," she said to Cassandra, hurriedly stacking away the last of the lunch plates.

"Where are we going now?" the child asked with a sigh. Then, brightening, "Are we following Ondott and Hundi?"

"No, we're going to see Barbara and Stephen," her mother responded, thinking, "That sounded a lot more confident than I feel!"

This seemed to satisfy the child, "Okay," she said, then, "Its jolly hot, I think I'll give Daisy a bath in the sink." Daisy was her favourite doll.

Daphne warned her against making a mess or using too much water, then went to start the engine.

It had been warm in the cabin and outside the sun beat down mercilessly, the boat's steelwork too hot to touch. Daphne lifted the wooden deckboard and pulled at the recoil rope which started the little engine.

"One day I'll be able to afford a proper diesel engine, and just press a button," she thought wryly, but the Volvo Penta roared into life at the first pull, then settled to a gentle purr as she eased the throttle to tickover.

Soon the *'Owl & the Pussycat'* was nosing out of the basin, under the ring-road and on up the mainline to Horseley Fields Junction, where the Wyrley and Essington Canal branched off to the left. The first thing Daphne noticed, after she had steered her boat onto its new course, was the clarity of the water. Expecting a muddy soup, she was amazed to clearly see the bed of the canal, and vast shoals of quite large fish darting hither and thither under the hull.

Old warehouses lined the banks, their aging brickwork disappearing vertically into the water. Daphne imagined the old working boats once lining up to collect cargo alongside these now derelict structures, incongruous against a modern backdrop of tower blocks and prefabricated office space.

Further on, she spotted a crowd of youths on the towpath, messing with an old moped. Her heart beat a little more quickly as the boat drew closer to them, but they hardly noticed the *"Owl & the Pussycat'* cruise by, and her journey continued uneventfully, until the wharf at Wednesfield came into view.

Hundi Mostrarskegg otherwise known as George, had been right about the petrol station. It was just across the road from the canal. Breathing a sigh of relief that all had gone smoothly, Daphne stowed the cans of fuel under the sterndeck, paused to wipe the perspiration dripping from her brow, and steered the *'Owl & the Pussycat'* into the centre of the canal once more.

With Wednesfield far astern, Daphne relaxed more. It was really better than she had expected. Wasteland extended on either side of the canal, but trees grew close to the banks, affording a measure of shade from the, now burning, sun. She found it fun, never knowing what waited around each bend, as the waterway twisted, first one way and then the other, following the contours of the landscape. She came to understand why boaters nicknamed this canal, the 'Curly Wyrley'.

Rounding just such a bend, she noticed a large, bulky object floating in the water ahead. It was too large to pass, and at first Daphne struggled to identify what it could be. She throttled back, allowing the *"Owl & the Pussycat'* to edge closer, until she recognized a large, three-seater settee, complete with cushions, bobbing gently up and down. It straddled the canal, but a gentle nudge from the bow caused it to rotate and allow the boat to brush past.

"The things people throw in the canal around here," she thought lightly, pleased with herself for negotiating the obstacle so efficiently.

Engrossed in self-congratulation, while navigating another bend she failed to notice the two matching armchairs, and hit first one and then the other, with resounding thumps.

"A complete three-piece suite!" she exclaimed, incredulously, "Whatever next?"

The *'Owl & the Pussycat'* nudged aside the household furniture and cruised placidly on her way. The canal was quiet. Local residents sought shelter from the heat of the day. No other boats were about, and only the occasional individual ventured along the towpath.

Eventually, the trees gave way to flat grassland stretching back from the canal banks, and in the distance rose blocks of flats and tenement houses. The occasional bridge carried minor roads over the canal, and while approaching one of these, Daphne heard the distant roar of traffic. Consulting the guidebook, she guessed the sound came from the busy M6 Motorway, which fetched a congratulatory smile to her lips, as she knew the canal crossed under the motorway, and then it was just a short distance to Sneyd Junction and the Water Board's yard.

The *'Owl & the Pussycat'* began to nose through the narrows of an old stone bridgehole. Then, with a sudden shudder, the boat stopped dead. At first Daphne thought they had run aground, but in the clear water she saw that the bottom lay a good two feet beneath the hull. Revving the engine, first forward, then in reverse, had no effect. The *'Owl & the Pussycat'* refused to budge.

"Maybe something's stuck under the boat," thought the girl, and reached for the long, heavy, boatpole on the cabin roof. She ran the engine full ahead, and poled against the canal bottom for all she was worth, but to no avail. Then she tried full reverse, and ran to the bows to pole from there. The boat moved back about a foot and then stopped dead again. Daphne wiped perspiration from her face and threw the pole back on the roof in disgust.

Cassandra poked her head out of the cabin, "Why have we stopped here, Mummy?" Daphne, lying on the back deck trying to peer under the boat, muttered that they were stuck.

Cassandra leaned over the side, "Mummy," she said matter-or-factly, "there's a door in the bottom of the canal."

"Don't be silly!" Daphne was in no mood for games. The hot sun was wreaking havoc with her patience, "Have you been reading 'Alice in Wonderland' again?"

"But, Mummy," the child insisted, "there is…under the boat, look!"

With a frustrated sigh, Daphne decided to play along with the child's fantasy, hoping she would quickly tire of the game and return to the cabin. Then, she looked over to where Cassandra was pointing, and saw the front door from someone's house wedged under the hull.

Lying lightly on the bottom as the boat passed over, the suction created must have lifted one edge, just enough to wedge the door against the rudder post. A hard thwack with the boatpole quickly released it, to sink gently back to the canal bed once more. Daphne towed the *'Owl & the Pussycat'* through the bridgehole with the bow rope, rather than risk running the engine and getting stuck again.

After rewarding Cassandra with a couple of biscuits, and fetching a sandwich for herself, she once more set the boat onwards up the canal.

"Well," she thought, grimly, "a three piece suite and a front door…I suppose the next thing will be the kitchen sink!"

A huge, concrete bridge structure, carrying the busy motorway over the water, came into view beyond the next bend, and the girl knew that the Water Board yard was just beyond. They would stop there and clean up, have something more substantial to eat. It was close to three o'clock and, hopefully, another three hours would see them at their final destination.

Daphne's eyes stung with perspiration. She had difficulty focusing. The water surface ahead appeared broken, unnatural. She wiped her eyes and looked again, but it still looked peculiar. The little wavelets rippling the surface stopped abruptly fifty yards ahead, and the water looked at once still, but choppy.

As the *'Owl & the Pussycat'* motored nearer to this phenomenon, Daphne was not sure whether to slow down, or just press on through. The boat was almost at the edge of the ripples before she realized what was causing this strange appearance of the water. With a cry of despair, she rushed to the throttle and threw the Volvo Penta into reverse, but it was too late. The boat's forward momentum carried it on until the propeller became entangled and the engine died. The *'Owl & the Pussycat'* floated silently and forlornly on a sea of thick, choking weed that stretched into the distance as far as the eye could see.

Daphne could only stare, horrified. "So, this is it," she thought. "This is as far as we go. There's no way the engine will take us through that lot."

Hot, tired, hungry and depressed, the girl slumped onto the stern deckboard, defeated. Tears of frustration welled up and she began to sob. Fate had abruptly turned triumph to disaster, and it was too much for her to bear. Then she turned, conscious of a pair of curious eyes watching from the bank. A dishevelled, grubby urchin, in shorts and tee-shirt, and wearing an old school cap, stood motionless on the towpath. Daphne judged he was about ten years old.

The urchin realized she was looking at him, "Wha'sa marrer wiv yer?" he asked, then, "'Ay, missus, der yer know tha' boot's the wron' colour?"

Daphne leapt to her feet, "How far does this weed stretch?" she shouted at the urchin, who looked dumbly back at her for a moment, before replying, "I doon' knaw," his mucky brow furrowed as he thought hard, then, "Al'mos' ter t' junction, I thin'."

She checked the guidebook, "The one just ahead, Sneyd Junction?"

The urchin shook his head, "Na, the nex' un…near L'more School."

Daphne found Leamore School marked on her map, by the junction with the Walsall Canal, a couple of miles further on. "You mean Birchills Junction? Where the Walsall Canal meets this one?"

The urchin nodded, "Aye...m' school's jus' be there."

"And it's clear past there?"

The urchin nodded again.

"Thanks!" Daphne leapt to her feet, all previous depression evaporated. If the boy was right, the weeded stretch only lasted a mile or so. It may not be possible, but if she could push the boat through the weed with the long boatpole, as far as Sneyd Junction and the Water Board's yard, maybe the workers there would be able to help her. Surely they must have a dredger, or some sort of machinery? But she would have to hurry. It was already three-thirty, and she had no idea when they finished work for the day.

She grabbed the long pole from the cabin roof, and sinking one end into the canal, threw her weight onto the other. The *'Owl & the Pussycat'* begrudgingly slid a few feet further into the weed.

It was going to be hard, slow work...and hot, oh, so hot!

Cassandra appeared from the cabin wanting to know what was happening. Daphne hardly had the breath to explain, and sent the child back inside to fetch an old towel so she could wipe her face.

Eventually, almost exhausted by her efforts, Daphne poled the boat under the motorway bridge, where lack of light caused the weed to grow more sparsely, and out into the hot sunshine on the other side, where it quickly thickened up again. Sneyd Junction was only a few hundred yards away, but it seemed to take forever before the old quayside appeared ahead, with the Water Board buildings beyond.

The urchin on the towpath had long since disappeared and the area seemed eerily quiet. She continued to pole, pausing occasionally to rest and wipe the perspiration now steadily dripping from her brow. The weed was thick right up to the quayside, and Daphne concentrated on moving the boat through the water as quickly as possible. At last, the bow bumped against the stonework. It was only then she looked up and realized that fate had, once again, dealt her a losing hand.

The buildings were derelict; windows smashed, tiles missing from the roof, the concrete frontage cracked and holed. Obviously, no-one had worked there for many years. Daphne looked about, and for the first time felt a tremor of fear. It was no place to spend the night. On the far side of the canal lay a field with one piebald horse, mangy and flea-bitten. To the rear was wasteland, and a now distant motorway; beyond that the outline of tower-block flats. Further on, the canal made a sharp, hairpin bend to the right and she saw the metallic roofs of tinkers' caravans glinting in the afternoon sun.

No, it was not a place to linger long. She checked her watch, already knowing it was after five o'clock. The sun was losing its intense heat, and beginning to descend.

"About three and a half hours of daylight," Daphne calculated, desperately trying not to panic.

No-one was about, but that could change at any time. She had two stark choices; go on or go back. The thought of a return journey didn't appeal. They would never make Wolverhampton Basin before dark, and she had seen nowhere that looked a safe, overnight mooring. Surely, if the urchin was right and the weed only extended to Leamore School, poling for an hour or so should see them through and into clear water; but suppose he were wrong, or deliberately lying? Perhaps there was more weed further on…eventually they would run out of daylight…

Cassandra demanded dinner.

Daphne made her decision. They would spend no more than half an hour at the derelict yard; have some food and a drink. Then, she would clear the obstruction from around the propeller so the engine would be ready to work when required, and pole the boat out of the weed, or till darkness made it impossible to proceed further. She took solace from the fact that, if the weed didn't end, then the boat would sit in mid-canal all night, where at least no-one could get to them.

Feeling much better now her plan was defined, Daphne ushered Cassandra back into the cabin and set about preparing a meal.

Once they had eaten, and Cassandra pronounced herself satisfied, Daphne left her to wash the dinner dishes, and lifted the board on the sterndeck to begin the task of clearing the propeller.

It was a backbreaking job. When the boat was built, Daphne could not afford the luxury of a diesel engine, so the boatbuilder had, somewhat begrudgingly, modified the weed-hatch specifically designed for access to a propeller, and fitted the Volvo Penta into it.

Consequently, it was necessary to unfasten the engine securing brackets and lift the outboard out of the weedhatch, before the propeller could be reached. Daphne had only done it once before, when a plastic bag got caught up whilst taking on water at the marina. It was a difficult job then, but today she was tired, and the outboard motor was heavy. It took all her strength, hauling it up far enough to get a hand down the leg and feel for the tangle of weeds caught in the propeller blades. Fortunately, the stems were not very tough and came away without much effort. Sighing with relief, she dropped the engine back into the weedhatch and made it secure.

Now there was just time to fetch a long, cool drink from the cabin, and they would be on their way again.

A distant drone of motorway traffic initially obscured the thud-thud of the big marine diesel engine. Daphne was inside the boat when her ears pricked up to the noise, rapidly approaching from around the hairpin bend. She rushed on deck, though at first nothing was visible. Then, to her utter amazement and delight, a Water Board dredger appeared, swathing its way through the weed and clearing a channel as effortlessly as a hot knife through butter.

The men on board saw her and slowed their engine. "You alright, love?" shouted one.

"I am now!" the girl responded, "How is the weed further on?"

"You'll do fine from here," the man shouted back, "we've cleared it right through to Brownhills."

"Thank you!" Daphne called, excitedly, "You've made my day."

"Happy to oblige!" the man responded, opening his throttle once more. The thud-thud of the diesel quickened, and a froth spewed from under the stern as the dredger picked up speed.

Daphne had no wish to obstruct the propeller again, so carefully poled her boat through the weed and into the channel left by the dredger, before starting the engine. The Volvo Penta fired up first pull, and soon the water was gurgling under the hull as the *'Owl & the Pussycat'* once more pursued her journey up the Wyrley and Essington Canal.

The dredger men were right. Within a mile, all the weed had disappeared and the waterway was completely open. Daphne breathed a prayer to the gods that nothing further would occur to upset their journey, then settled back for the last five or six miles to the junction with the Cannock Arm.

For the next hour and a half, they twisted and turned through some of the shabbiest areas in the Midlands. Daphne wrinkled her nose at the Harden sewage works, and kept as far from the towpath as water depth would allow until they had passed the council houses of the, much dreaded, Goscote Estate. Moorers at Dixie's told tales of missiles hurled by the residents of Goscote Estate, and even one boat peppered with a shotgun.

On that summer evening, many were barbecuing in their gardens, and Daphne made a point of waving a friendly hand, and smiling as she went past. To her surprise, they all waved cheerily back, though some shouted that the boat was the wrong colour, as the blue and red *'Owl & the Pussycat'* cruised past them.

For once, Daphne felt content it was the only thing the Goscote residents were throwing her way. Before she knew it, the houses were dwindling, replaced by rough countryside and open fields. As the sun began to sink towards the western horizon, an iron bridge spanned the canal ahead of them, and a signpost pointed north, with the legend, 'Cannock Arm'.

The arm is two miles long and straight as an arrow. When the *'Owl & the Pussycat'* had negotiated the ninety degree turn, Daphne steered into the middle of the canal and opened the throttle again. It was a beautiful evening. The sun was low behind bankside trees to her left, lighting the canal with a diffuse orange glow. No wind stirred the tranquil surface, and her narrowboat steamed through the water like a train.

"Like she knows we're almost there." Daphne thought, gazing with immense pride at her jaunty little craft. She patted the cabin roof with affection, "Well done!" she whispered, "Well done!"

It was then she saw movement on the far towpath to her right. From the corner of her eye, she noticed a long, pole-like object rise up from out of the trees. Daphne at once recognized it as a fishing pole, and realized there were many of them outstretched across the water in front of her. In the half light it was only possible to make out a silhouette of the fishermen holding the poles, but obviously there was an evening match in progress.

Daphne eased back the throttle. The *'Owl & the Pussycat'* slowed to a more sedate pace, to not disturb the fish. Quieter now, the boat slid majestically up the canal, and the fishermen, each in their turn, lifted their poles to allow her passage.

To Daphne, the scene was reminiscent of medieval knights, lances raised in a gesture of tribute, as their liege passed by. It seemed, for all the world, like they were saluting the little boat for its courage and tenacity at the end of an epic voyage.

The first stars twinkled in the heavens as Daphne closed the throttle, and eased the *'Owl & the Pussycat'* alongside the big narrowboat, *'Strawberry Fields'*, moored at the top end of the Cannock Arm.

Barbara's head appeared from a side hatch, "Hi!' she shouted, "You've made it after all. Did you have a good trip?" Then, she screwed her eyes and perused the *'Owl & the Pussycat'*, "You know, dear…I've never noticed it until now…but has anyone ever told you, that boat is the wrong colour."

Daphne swallowed the last dregs of Viking Shandy from the tumbler in her hand and collected two empty bottles of mead from the cabin roof. She smiled contentedly. Somehow, it just didn't seem to matter anymore.

ELLIS GORDON'S PASSING

He first opened my office door on a wet, November afternoon; the sort of day when sensible people are by their firesides and definitely not thinking to buy a canal boat. Dixie's Marina was never at its best between November and March.

I was playing 'solitaire' on the computer and pondering the possibility of sneaking a few days away from my desk to relieve the boredom. It was always a quiet time in the boating industry. Autumn colours had long since metamorphosed to the dismal grey of winter. Beyond my office window a plethora of sheeted hulls nudged softly against dank, slippery jetties, waiting out the bleak depressive months until Easter warmth once more stirred their owners' attentiveness.

Ellis Gordon stood a tall man, well over six feet, and slim though not skinny. His face held the wrinkles of a long-term smoker and his eyes crinkled; soft, brown, and smiling. He was a man you trusted from the first moment, an instant friend, in a way few people ever can be. Thirty years in the police service had taken him no further than station sergeant, for that was exactly as far as he wanted to go.

The bitterness, cynicism, and intolerance so rife in a profession handling the most sordid of human activities, had left no apparent mark on Ellis Gordon. If you mislaid a beloved dog, or wallet, or wristwatch, he was the officer you wanted to find at the reception desk; the one that assured you your personal tragedy was his also, not just another inconvenience requiring yet more endless reams of paperwork.

Ellis had left the police force behind when he first stepped into my office with his wife Miranda, that November afternoon. At age fifty-two, he had chosen early retirement to pursue his lifelong dream and own a canal boat.

Miranda Gordon served as the perfect foil for Ellis. A few years younger than her husband, round-faced and gentle, her soft smile belied a streak of practicality acquired from a lifetime in the nursing profession. It was soon evident this couple had each learned their place in the relationship and rode it comfortably within a framework of enduring love and companionship.

Two hours following our first meeting, Ellis and Miranda became the proud owners of a luxury, thirty-two foot, canal cruiser and I was arranging a marina mooring to accommodate them.

Not that it was an easy sale. Ellis's enthusiasm carried us on a tour round every purchasable craft on the marina. I noted he spent just long enough on each to smoke a cigarette, before pursing his lips and assessing that the vessel just failed to meet their needs. We inspected a dozen boats, and he consumed best part of a pack, before deciding on the thirty-two footer that had initially attracted their attention.

From then on, the Gordon's spent all their leisure hours at the marina. Miranda worked as a theatre sister in a busy city hospital and could spare only a day or two each week, so it was mostly during those times when she was off-duty that I would see their boat, "Dabchick", nosing in or out of the marina. Occasionally, Ellis visited the boat without his wife, but never passed my office without calling in for a chat. I soon learned he seldom shook hands. Only a hug was good enough for his friends, and it was a welcome hug, a hug of warmth and love that oozed from every pore of the man. It was nothing sexual, you understand, just a loving, caring hug of friendship that never failed to make my day the better for it happening.

Ellis's visits to my office grew more frequent during those short, damp days when often no-one else would appear at all, and if the telephone rang it was merely someone desperate to sell insurance or advertising space. His became a special friendship. I began to relish the prospect of his face peering in through my window, checking I was not busy, before he entered.

He was the only visitor for which the large, red 'NO SMOKING' notice on the wall above my head held no authority. Eventually I acquired an old, white plastic, ashtray just to avoid his need to intermittently rush outside and discard the ash. Such interruptions, while holding me spellbound amid tales of life in the police force, or as a young soldier in Malaya, were not to be brooked; for Ellis Gordon had a way with words that brought stories to life, lending them a colour and texture that made one wish they could go on forever.

It grew into something of a ritual: the face at the window; the open door; the bear hug, before flopping into his chair and squinting askance at the notice above my head.

"That wouldn't apply to me, would it?" he would ask with a half-grin, and I would grin back, pull the old plastic ashtray out of my drawer and slide it across the desk.

"Time you gave those things up," I would murmur, "before they give you up."

Ellis would pull a face and mutter something about, "… one day…" before sitting back, drawing deeply on the smoke and saying, "Did I ever tell you about Harry the Hatchetman from down Bromborough Docks..." or something similar, and yet another enthralling tale would commence to unfold from the lips of this Master of the Spoken Word.

After half an hour or so, he would remember Miranda's warning that lunch was in fifteen minutes, and there would be another swift bearhug and a hasty departure, leaving me to dispose of the six or seven smoked ends that had accumulated during his visit.

Miranda once assured me that his tardiness never concerned her. She simply gave Ellis a time, multiplied it by three in her own mind, and thus ensured the meal was at its peak when he returned.

As spring nudged aside winter, the marina came alive once more and I saw much less of Ellis Gordon. Never a man to impose, he seemed to sense that I no longer had the time for long chats and story telling. He would still call by occasionally, smoke a few cigarettes and hear me scold him for his habit, but he never outstayed his welcome, and sometimes there was just the huge hug, and he was back out the door and on his way.

The summer passed as every other boating season at the marina. There were the usual petty squabbles between the moorers. The sales row thrived, and I would have a constant headache finding berths for boats purchased by the continuous stream of newcomers to the inland waterways. Dixie's had never been so popular, the canal system never so well used, the cash tills never so busy. But, as always it couldn't go on forever. Summer transposed to the gold and yellow of autumn, to be rapidly replaced by the gloomy grey of winter days once more. Boats were sheeted, moorers departed, and Ellis Gordon returned to lighten my winter boredom.

A new subject now dominated this ex-policeman's repertoire, and I might have cringed had anyone but he held forth on stories of damaged lockgates, tidal waves, and the plethora of canal-related tales already relayed to me innumerable times throughout the season by those who'd passed through my office door before him. When Arthur Higginbottom wedged his forty-five footer in the second lock at Calveston Junction on a Saturday morning, and caused twenty hire-boats to miss the deadline and lose their deposits, it was guaranteed I would hear the story a zillion times from over-enthusiastic moorers returning to the marina on a Sunday afternoon.

Hardly a summer weekend went by that didn't produce some minor catastrophe or comic occurrence, rapidly converted to temporary folklore until done to death by too much exposure, or simply overshadowed by an even juicier fillip. I heard it all, over and over, each excited individual assuming his was the scoop, the headline banner to rock me from my deskbound apathy.

Not that I minded. It was good to keep in touch, and I fostered my association with Dixie's moorers, both as a business strategy and a personal pleasure. Re-hashing old news already done to death was not my first choice for a wet, winter afternoon, unless of course, the storyteller was Ellis Gordon.

Consequently, after three weeks went by in February and Ellis's face appeared not once framed in my office window, I became more than a little concerned. The influenza virus had been particularly active that winter and I consoled myself with thoughts that he was probably confined to bed, and at least in good hands, given his spouse's chosen profession.

Miranda Gordon finally entered my office a few days later. I was relieved when told that Ellis was in the marina shop and on his way to join us. My enquiry as to their prolonged absence elicited the response that he had been unwell, but wished to tell me about it himself. I had little time to wait, for there was the wrinkled face at the window, the opened door, the familiar bear-hug, and Ellis was in the chair and enquiring of my health.

I saw at once that he was somewhat gaunt. A touch of grey infused his pallor, as anyone recovering from a bad attack of 'flu. It was not until a full five minutes had elapsed and the old plastic ashtray still lay concealed in my drawer, that I knew something serious was amiss with Ellis Gordon.

It was almost matter-of-fact, in the same casual, relaxed way he related his mesmerizing stories, that I learned his life was almost over, ebbing rapidly from a large, inoperable carcinoma in his left lung.

One glance at Miranda told me quicker than words that there was nothing medical science could do, bar go through the motions. A lifetime nursing cancer patients admirably qualified her to recognize the ones that had a chance, and those who were doomed. Her eyes told me emphatically that Ellis was the latter.

He said, "I guess you could say, I told you so….." to which I stammered, "I-I wouldn't dream…" and felt that I was taking the news far worse than he was.

He smiled, "Then you won't mind fetching that ashtray out of your drawer?"

My look of horror caused the smile to broaden, as he simply said, "A bit too late to think of giving up now."

I only saw Ellis Gordon three times more. The last occasion was on the marina forecourt. Miranda had brought him out for a run in the car, and when it was obvious he was too weak even for a hug, I knew I would never see him at the marina again.

I was away on holiday the day he died. They rang me from the marina with the news. I returned in time for the funeral, but did not go. I knew it would be well attended. Most of the county police force would be there. Instead, I just sat at my desk and thought about the man who had come to mean so much to me. The face peering in the window, the way he flopped into his chair, the stories that he told so well. Most of all the bear-hugs; those wonderful, loving, intimate embraces that let you know how this man truly was your friend.

His place in Heaven was reserved, I felt sure of that. My mind's eye visualized Ellis Gordon, in his usual manner, greeting Saint Peter with an enormous bear-hug. Unable to suppress a wry grin, I thought, "There'll be a few angels with crumpled wings in Heaven tonight."

Pausing only to brush away an errant tear, I dragged the old plastic ashtray from its drawer and tossed it unceremoniously into the waste-bin.

DAPHNE'S DILEMMA.

Daphne Forbes-Jackson secured the mooring lines, shut off the engine, and breathed a long sigh of relief, mingled with satisfaction. There were two distinct reasons for the sigh. Firstly, her narrowboat, *'Owl & the Pussycat'* had just completed a long cruise down the Wyrley and Essington Canal from Pelsall Junction, and all the way back to Dixie's Marina without any mishap whatever, although persistent jibes that the little red and blue narrowboat really ought to be pea-green, from virtually every boater she passed, had become more and more irksome. The second reason for her sigh of relief was on noticing the empty berth over on the next pontoon, where the bearded guy usually moored his boat.

Ever since her narrowboat's tunnel light had illumined him in an embarrassing situation with an unknown woman under the old railway bridge a few weeks back - and just because she'd mentioned it in passing to old May Trumpton on *'August Moon'*, who'd blabbed it around the marina and then some - the bearded guy had been giving her dark looks each time their paths crossed. At least, for this evening, she could relax and not worry about possible harassment.

Cassandra had been unusually quiet and unresponsive over the last few days. Though ever an introvert child, Daphne sensed more than her daughter's customary moodiness, and guessed it was her imminent return to school after the long summer break, that was upsetting the seven year old.

This would be her third term since they moved onto the boat. Prior to that, she had always enjoyed school, but Daphne knew that some of the other children taunted her, called her 'gypsy' because she lived on the canal.

Once, on their way back from Pelsall Junction, Cassandra had asked, "Mummy, when are we going to live in a house again?"

Daphne enjoyed living afloat. She had never been so happy in her life and the thought of moving back into a house or flat appalled her. It was lovely at the marina, quiet and peaceful, and she got on really well with the other moorers - all, apart from the bearded guy, that is.

It was time to go below and cook Cassandra's supper, but Daphne paused for a final glance about her. In the late summer evening Dixie's Marina shone, as low sunlight reflected from the red and gold leaves of trees around the perimeter. She noticed a yellow and blue boat that had not been there when they left ten days before. It was moored further down the pontoon, on an opposite jetty to the '*Owl & the Pussycat*', and looked very smart.

"About a forty-footer," Daphne thought, grinning to herself at this air of expertise. A few months ago she could not have told whether it was twenty foot, or sixty. She looked to see if anyone was on board. The curtains were open but there was no sign of life, although a wisp of wood smoke curled lazily from the saloon stovepipe.

"Someone having a late holiday, and moored up for the night," she thought, her curiosity fading before Cassandra's wail of hunger.

Three days later, there was still no sign of the bearded guy, and the yellow and blue narrowboat had not moved from its mooring. Smoke no longer curled from the chimney and Daphne saw no-one go near it, though she was so busy coercing Cassandra into preparing for school that she may easily have missed a casual visitor. Even a trip into town, the purchase of new school uniform, a fizzy drink and sticky bun, failed to raise a modicum of enthusiasm from the unfortunate child.

Daphne, nerves frayed by Cassandra's constant sulks, eventually lost her temper and shouted at the child to pull herself together, which did no good at all and just made worse the underlying guilt Daphne was feeling. She found herself glancing in the windows of estate agents, and the 'Homes for Sale' sections of local newspapers; activities destined to infect her with a depression comparable to her daughter's.

Late Saturday afternoon, two days before Cassandra's return to school, Daphne heard a diesel engine churning the marina silt, and looking out of the cabin window glimpsed the bearded guy returning to his mooring. Her heart sank. She had found herself vehemently hoping he had gone for good, although she knew that was extremely unlikely.

It was not that she was frightened of him, but she really wanted to avoid confrontation. The bearded guy was short and skinny with the makings of a pot-belly, and a pointy beard that wiggled up and down when he talked. Daphne had long ago learned to take care of herself in those difficult moments when men find it hard to accept an attractive woman telling them, "No!" She could handle that sort of situation, but it was his sheer arrogance and creepiness that disgusted her, and made her flesh crawl whenever he was near.

"Well, if he causes me any problems, he'd better look out or he'll be in the canal," she thought fiercely, though at the same time hoping fervently that he would not.

Cassandra was still down in the dumps. The previous night Daphne had tackled her once more, in an attempt to solicit what was wrong with the child. Eventually, Cassandra burst into tears, stating that she hated school, had no friends, and was tormented by everyone because she was a gypsy.

No amount of logical reasoning by her mother softened the little girl's anguish. She hated the canals, loathed the marina, and abhorred the *'Owl & the Pussycat'*. Nothing, short of living in a house, would make her happy again.

Daphne knew all the hate and loathing was false. Cassandra had been blissfully happy on the boat all summer, until school suddenly loomed once more. But there seemed no strategy to overcome the bullying. Last term, Daphne had visited the Headmistress, but while she was sympathetic and promised to do all she could to stop the taunting, it had continued unabated.

The only option was to sell the *'Owl & the Pussycat'* and move ashore. With heavy heart, Daphne made a mental note to call on the marina manager next day, and obtain an estimate of what the boat might fetch on the open market. She knew it would not be enough to purchase a house, but perhaps somewhere not *too* ghastly for rent......

A sudden loud rap on the cabin door jerked her from this depressive train of thought. Cassandra was in bed. It was twilight outside. Who would come calling at that hour? It could only be the bearded guy spoiling for a fight...well, he was going to get one...she was just in the mood...

"Why the hell don't you just stay away from me?" She shouted, throwing open the door to the back deck with a bang, "I'm sick to death of....oh...sorry..."

The man standing on the jetty was not the bearded guy. He was tall and quite good-looking, about her age or a little older, and he regarded her calmly with a mischievous twinkle in his eyes.

"I'm sorry to trouble you," he said. "You were obviously expecting someone else? Well......I hope you were." His smile was quite disarming, so unlike the bearded guy's leer. "I just wondered if you had a drop of milk to spare. My fridge is on the blink and, well...I think it's turned mine to cheese."

"I...I...I'm so sorry!" Daphne stammered, feeling acutely embarrassed, "Yes, yes, of course. I'll just get some."

The man handed her a small enamel jug, "Just enough for a cup of tea before bed," he said, then almost as an afterthought, "and perhaps one in the morning, if you have enough to spare."

Daphne filled the jug, wondering who on earth was this stranger? She knew most of the moorers, by sight at least, but she had never seen him before.

"There you are," she said, "It's full to the brim. I have plenty."

The man reached out, "Thanks very much." He took the jug from her hand. "You've saved my life. I'm useless without a cup of tea, especially first thing in the morning. I'll be sure and return it tomorrow." He turned to leave, then hesitated, "By the way, I'm James Erin. I haven't been here long.....still finding my way around."

Daphne introduced herself. "Are you moored here?" she asked. It was an innocuous question, though part of her hoped he would say 'yes'.

James Erin nodded, "I've spent the last few weeks cruising up from the South-East; arrived here six days ago. I start a new job on Monday." He pointed back down the pontoon, "That's my boat, *'Erin's Isle'*, the yellow and blue forty-footer over there." He grinned, a little abashed, "It's a bit of a play on words...the name, you see...?"

Daphne smiled back, "Yes," she laughed, "I see. Do you live aboard?"

The man nodded, "Yes, and I love it. I've been afloat for two years now; much better than living in a house."

He thanked Daphne once more for the milk, and she watched him walk back down the pontoon and onboard *'Erin's Isle'*. A curl of wood smoke once more drifted lazily from the saloon stovepipe.

"He seems a nice man." She closed the cabin door, any further thoughts of James Erin soon overtaken by the darker, more immediate problems besetting her. Finally, overwhelmed and frustrated by her dilemma, Daphne decided on an early night, but it was a long time before sleep came. She lay awake, tossing and turning, her mind remorselessly seeking a solution that would placate her daughter's feelings, yet allow them to remain on the *'Owl & the Pussycat'*. No answer was forthcoming, and finally she drifted into fitful sleep.

Next morning, immediately following breakfast, Daphne made sure Cassandra was safely inside the boat before walking determinedly down the marina to the Sales Office. The manager was not about, but a young sales lad who knew the boat gave her an idea of the price it might fetch. It was less than she had expected, though as the boy said, she would have got more with a proper diesel engine fitted, but with only an outboard motor...he sucked in his breath...well, everyone wanted a proper diesel, didn't they?

Daphne had not been able to afford a diesel engine, so the boatyard had fitted an old outboard under the sterndeck temporarily, until she had more money available. That time had not yet arrived, and so the resale value was much lower than she had anticipated.

She told the lad she would think about it, and strolled slowly back up the marina walkway, wondering just what she was going to do. Deep inside, she knew there was only one answer. Cassandra's welfare was the most important thing in the world to her. It was tearing her apart to see the child so frightened and miserable. She would sell the *'Owl & the Pussycat'*, cut her losses, and find a flat or small house for rent in the town.

She turned; retraced her steps to the marina office.

The lad seemed unperturbed by this quick return and produced the necessary forms with apathetic ease. "When can it be brought down to the sales row?" he asked, as she began filling in the requested details, the enormity of what she was doing only slowly dawning.

"Oh!" She hadn't thought of that. "Can we still live aboard, if it's on the sales row?"

The lad shook his head firmly, "Nope," he said, "'gainst the rules. We can't show people over it if yer aboard, can we?"

"But…" Daphne was flummoxed, "…I can't afford to move off until it's sold."

The lad shook his head again, more languidly this time. It wasn't his problem. Then he must have noticed Daphne's chagrin, "Tell yer what," he said, "We'll keep it on the books, an' if anyone's interested, we'll send them up to yer. As long as yer don' mind showin' people over?"

Daphne brightened, "Oh, no," she said, "That'll be fine. I'm usually on board."

After reluctantly setting her signature to the brokerage agreement she walked slowly back up the marina towards the *'Owl & the Pussycat'*, noticing all those things to which she had become so accustomed, and grown to love. The distant cheery voice of a boater negotiating Chumpley Lock; Ken, the groundsman, cutting grass around the shower block with his little tractor; the lowing of George Anderson's milkers in the next field. Soon, she would be leaving it all behind for the hustle and bustle of life in the big town, the snarling roar of traffic, the crowds of shoppers, the pressures and stresses of so-called 'normal' living.

Out of the blue, Daphne felt her emotions begin to overwhelm her. She quickened her step along the pontoon, determined to seek shelter in the *'Owl & the Pussycat'* before the inevitable tears. At first she pretended not to hear the voice hailing her. Another dozen strides and she would be within the boat's cabin and able to vent her grief away from prying eyes, but after two more steps she stopped and turned, good manners preventing further pretence at deafness. She realized the yellow and blue boat, *'Erin's Isle'*, was to her left, and its owner was standing on the foredeck.

"I hope I didn't startle you?" James Erin looked concerned. "I just wanted to return your milk," he continued, "I went into town this morning to do some shopping. If you can wait a moment, I'll get it for you?"

He mustn't see her like this! Even as she hesitated, the tears began to well up. "Tha'…that's ok," she blurted, "I have to go. I…I've left Cassandra alone on the boat. I'll come and get it later."

Head down, she almost ran the last few yards, went quickly inside the cabin and sank down on the little settee, sobbing uncontrollably into the cushions.

Cassandra showed grave concern for her mother's unhappiness. She sat with her arm around Daphne, demanding to know the cause of such intense grief. Daphne had already determined she would say nothing of her plans until the boat was sold. She didn't wish to raise the child's hopes before a sale was finalised, and found herself searching for some excuse to explicate this show of emotion.

"It's nothing, darling," she sobbed, "Mummy just feels a little poorly this morning, that's all."

"If that bearded man's been hurting you, I'll…" Cassandra looked very fierce.

"No, no, Cassie! No, it wasn't him, honestly. I haven't seen him for ages." Daphne felt quite shocked. She hadn't realized Cassandra was aware of any antagonism between her mother and the bearded guy, "It's amazing what children pick up on," she thought, making a valiant attempt to pull herself together, "Now, Cassie, do you have everything ready for school tomorrow?"

The little girl pulled a face, but nodded.

Later, when the tears were gone and her face repaired sufficient for public display, Daphne sat out on the sterndeck, breathing in the afternoon sunshine and absorbing the hustle and bustle of late season moorers squeezing the last ounce of pleasure from a summer soon to turn into long, dreary, inactive days of winter. Already the nights were growing longer. In just a few more weeks the inevitable winterising and sheeting down would begin. Boats would be emptied, cars loaded with the flotsam and jetsam left over from salad day activities, and Dixie's Marina would once again become the exclusive reserve of a few residential moorers who were already 'home'.

Daphne enjoyed winters at the marina; the little potbelly stove warming the cabin continuously from September till April; waking up to the magical stillness of a winter's morning; crisp, cold sunshine and frosted jetties, or the wild, wet and windy days when the *'Owl & the Pussycat'* tugged and harried at her mooring ropes, and it felt good to be snug and dry inside.

Daphne knew she was unlikely to experience such again. Before long, her days at Dixie's Marina would be just a memory, to be pigeon-holed, put aside and only brought out for inspection during rare moments of aloneness when such memories are lifted down, inspected, polished, and returned until another day. Cassandra would be happy, and do well at school, and that was all that mattered. Eventually, Daphne knew her daughter would fly the nest, get a job and a place of her own, leaving her free to pick up her life again and do as she wished. Maybe even buy another boat…

"Maybe," she mused, "maybe…"

A hollow clatter of footsteps on the pontoon terminated her reverie. She glanced up, shocked to see the bearded guy watching her intently, his manner menacing and abrupt.

"Wanted a word with you, Lady Muck!" he snapped, lurching across the deck towards her. The smell of stale alcohol assailed her nostrils. She felt herself back away, involuntarily, her breath coming in short gasps.

"Oh, go away!" she cried, "You're drunk! Get off my boat. Leave me alone!"

"You've caused me no end of problems," the bearded guy snarled, reaching out to grab her arm, "It's time someone taught you to keep your mouth shut."

Daphne dodged his wild lunge, placed two hands in the centre of his chest and pushed with all her strength, forcing him backwards onto the short jetty to which the *'Owl & the Pussycat'* was moored. The bearded guy had obviously not expected such resistance, and the sheer power of Daphne's thrust, coupled with a surfeit of alcohol, sent him staggering backwards, completely off balance.

All the frustrations of the last weeks poured out of Daphne, fuelling her anger. She followed up the offensive, once more catching him full in the chest with both hands, while the bearded guy vainly attempted to regain his equilibrium. This second attack eradicated any possibility of her opponent remaining upright. He staggered rapidly backwards down the short jetty, legs flailing in a futile attempt to catch up with the rest of his body. The legs may have succeeded had the jetty been somewhat longer, but on reaching the end they floundered wildly at fresh air before disappearing, along with their owner, into five feet of water.

Many of the boats in the immediate area were occupied, their owners utilizing one of the last Sundays of the season to make final preparations for winter. The sudden commotion, followed by a loud splash, caused heads to pop out of hatches and doorways all over the marina. The bearded guy's wife, herself curious of the strange noises, stepped out onto the foredeck of their boat, just in time to see her husband's head emerge from under the lagoon, spitting and coughing up muddy canal water.

Grins and jeers greeted the bearded guy as he broke surface and struck out for the land. He was not the most popular man at the marina. Wisely deciding to give the *'Owl & the Pussycat'* a wide berth, he half swam, half walked the short distance to an empty jetty further down the pontoon, where with much wheezing and coughing, he hauled himself from the water. Without a backward glance towards Daphne, he squelched off towards his own boat and a wife whose facial expression was anything but welcoming.

"Well! Won by a knock-out! Is this the standard Sunday afternoon entertainment at Dixie's, or just a one-off performance?"

Daphne had been concentrating on the bearded guy and had not noticed James Erin walk up the pontoon behind her. "I only came to return the milk," he continued, smiling and holding out a bottle.

Daphne reached out and took it, "Thank you."

"Are you alright?" His concern was genuine.

She nodded, regaining some composure, "Yes, I'm fine now. He startled me, though. I knew he wasn't a very nice man, but I didn't think he got drunk."

"From what I've heard on the marina grapevine," James was grinning, "you've seen more of him than you'd wish to."

Daphne, relieved now the encounter was over, grinned back, "Yes, and it wasn't a pretty sight, believe me. I hope I never see him without his trousers again. In fact," her face grew serious, "I hope I never see any of him again."

"Oh, I doubt he'll bother you again. I think you won that one fair and square."

Cassandra suddenly appeared in the cabin doorway, her eyes wide with excitement, "Mummy! Guess what? I've just seen that bearded man swimming with all his clothes on. Why…what would he be doing in the water…? Oh…" she noticed James Erin standing on the sterndeck, and suddenly became very coy, "…hello…"

"This is Mister Erin, Cassandra. He lives on the blue and yellow boat further down the pontoon."

"'*Erin's Isle*?" Cassandra thought for a moment, her brow furrowed, "Why is it your island?"

James Erin laughed, "Well," he said, "It's a little obscure… but a man named Shakespeare once wrote about a 'sea of trouble', and when I feel that all around me is troublesome, I can retire to my boat…my peaceful island in a troubled sea."

Cassandra was unimpressed, "Umm…" she said, and then turned to her mother, "Has the bearded man drowned?"

"Daphne laughed, "No, darling, he climbed out safely and has gone back to his boat."

Cassandra wrinkled her nose, "Pity," she said, matter-of-factly, and with a last sly glance at James Erin, went back to her cabin.

The man watched her go and smiled, "She seems a pleasant child."

"She can be a handful sometimes," Daphne responded, "She's at a difficult age."

James Erin laughed, "I think every age is difficult," he said, then grinned widely, "thirty-two, especially"

"Is that how old you are?"

"I will be, tomorrow." He sighed, "It's my birthday."

"Oh! Many happy returns for tomorrow," Daphne cried, "You don't look your age."

"Thank you, kind lady, but at such an advanced state of maturity it's best forgotten." He turned, about to go back to his boat, "I'd best get back. I start work tomorrow and I've stacks of preparation to do. If you're certain you're alright?"

Daphne nodded, part of her wishing he would stay, but she said, "Oh, yes, I'm fine. Thanks again."

He took a few steps down the pontoon, then hesitated, "By the way, your boat has a really nice name. Did you choose it?"

"Thank you. Yes, I did."

"And the colour scheme…"

About to cross the deck to the cabin door, Daphne froze in her stride. "Oh, no," she thought, "please, please don't suggest it should be pea-green!"

"…is just right." James continued. "You know," he went on, "most people would have painted it pea-green, in line with Lear's poem, but you chose to use contrasting colours," he looked thoughtful for a moment, then smiled warmly, "I guess that means you're not 'most people'."

James Erin walked back towards his boat, leaving Daphne open-mouthed on the stern deck. She watched him clamber aboard *'Erin's Isle'* and disappear through the front doors, before collecting herself enough to make her own way into the *'Owl & the Pussycat's'* cabin, thinking as she went, "He really is a nice man…a very nice man."

Monday morning dawned bright, with the promise of another fine day. Raising a reluctant and unhappy Cassandra from her bunk, via the bathroom, into her uniform, through to the breakfast table, and out through the cabin door and onto the pontoon, before half-dragging her unwilling child towards the car park and the waiting school bus… all left Daphne little time to appreciate the weather.

Halfway down the pontoon, James Erin was just leaving his boat. Casual sweater and jeans had been replaced by a business suit and tie. Coupled to a tan leather briefcase, he looked every inch the calm and confident 'man about town'.

Daphne finally persuaded Cassandra up the steps and onto the bus. After a final wave to the departing vehicle, she turned to retrace her steps as James Erin was unlocking his car.

"Good morning," he called cheerily, nonchalantly throwing his briefcase onto the passenger seat.

Daphne was horribly conscious of her old pink housecoat, the lack of make-up and.....oh, damn, why hadn't she done more than tug at her hair with the comb this morning?

She smiled, self-consciously, "Good morning, James. Happy birthday! You're looking very smart today."

His grin was boyish, "Thanks," he said, "New job...I start this morning...got to make a good impression."

She wanted to ask his profession, but he was already half in the car, so she just said, "Good luck!" and watched as with a final wave, he followed the school bus out of the car park and she was suddenly left standing alone.

Returning to the *'Owl & the Pussycat'*, Daphne felt distracted by a blend of gloom and resignation. A similar mood had overtaken her the previous evening, following her scuffle with the bearded guy. She cleaned up the breakfast things, washed dishes mechanically, her mind drifting over the happenings of the preceding few weeks. She still fervently hoped Cassandra might resume a liking for school, but deep down knew it was not very likely, unless by some miracle the bullies found someone else to taunt.

Eventually, with a long sigh, Daphne sank down onto the settee with a cup of coffee, resolved to at least try and come to terms with her emotions.

An hour later, while still struggling with the complexities of her life, the sound of voices outside made her open the cabin door, where she found an elderly couple wandering up and down the jetty, inspecting the *"Owl & the Pussycat".*

He was a tall, thin, balding man with horn-rimmed spectacles. His wife was shorter, with a blue rinse and severe lips.

"We understand you're selling?" the man said. His gaze went past her and out over the lagoon, as though denying her presence, "The office sent us up here."

Before Daphne could respond with more than a nod, the woman said sharply, "It seems a bit overpriced, for what it is."

Daphne opened her mouth to remonstrate, but the man said quickly, "It doesn't even have a diesel engine, I understand?" His gaze had moved on now and was scrutinizing the car park.

"No...eh...I didn't have one fitted..." her voice trailed off as she realized neither of them appeared to be listening. The man wandered up towards the foredeck, and peered into Cassandra's cabin through the front doors. Daphne wished she'd tidied a little more that morning, but she had not expected prospective buyers so soon.

"I'd like to see inside," the woman stated abruptly.

"Eh, yes...come on down," Daphne invited, holding the door wider. Her eyes darted around the little saloon, but all looked in place.

The woman squeezed, with some difficulty, through the narrow doorway. Her husband followed, banging his head sharply on the steel framework as he did so.

"There's not much room, is there?" The man was rubbing his brow. Daphne could see a bright red weal materializing on his forehead.

"You have to adjust," she smiled gamely, "I banged my head a few times at first, but you soon get used to it." The words sounded lame, like she was making excuses for the *'Owl & the Pussycat'*.

The couple wandered through the cabin, inspecting this, criticising that. Daphne stood, feeling useless, knowing they had little interest in anything she said. The bathroom was too small, Cassandra's cabin would need ripping out, the little galley was badly arranged, and the woman stated she would never, ever, consider sleeping in "…..a bed as minute as that!"

Eventually, they shuffled their way back onto the jetty. The man still rubbed his forehead. Daphne felt some satisfaction that the weal was turning blue. Then, he addressed her, though his gaze once more scanned the lagoon, "Well, of course the price is way too high. You'll have to come down if you want to sell it."

"And the name!" his wife interjected, with more than a degree of haughtiness, "We'd have to change the name." She looked most disgusted, "Whoever heard of a boat called the *'Owl & the Pussycat'*? And, anyway it's the wrong colour." She leaned over towards Daphne with a smile saturated in condescension, "If you're going to call it that, my dear, you really need to paint it a nice pea-green."

Resisting an urge to smack the lady right in the middle of her supercilious smile, Daphne forced her lips into what she hoped was an acceptable response, though it felt more of a malevolent grimace, and nodded dumbly.

The pair wandered away down the pontoon, muttering, "Well, we do have others to see…" and "…not sure it's what we're looking for…"

Daphne retired to the cabin and closed the door, before giving way to rage and frustration.

"How dare they?" she screamed, throwing punches at the cushions on the settee to vent her anger, "How dare they criticise my lovely boat? Horrible people." She patted the cabin sides reverently, "I would never sell you to the likes of them."

But in her heart she knew that if they did decide to purchase, she would have little option but to accept.

"It's not very likely, though," she thought with a giggle, her anger abated and now able to view the comedy of the situation. She laughed out loud remembering the man's bruised forehead. "It serves him right!"

But later in the day her melancholy returned. The sale of the *'Owl & the Pussycat'* was inevitable. Whoever bought the boat, it would not be hers anymore. She would no longer be a part of the canal life she had grown to love. Once again her mind searched for other options, and found none.

When the school bus arrived back at Dixie's without Cassandra onboard, her melancholy turned to fear and apprehension.

The driver was reassuring. She was getting a lift back from one of the teachers and would be arriving anytime soon. Daphne was not to worry.

Daphne couldn't help worrying. What had gone wrong in school? Why would a teacher bring her home? She returned to the *'Owl & the Pussycat'*, but couldn't settle and kept going out onto the sterndeck, scanning the pontoon for any sign of her daughter's return.

Then, with huge relief, she saw Cassandra running up the pontoon towards the boat. The child arrived, breathless, and threw herself into her mother's arms, "Mummy, Mummy, school was the greatest today! It was so...oo... cool."

Daphne couldn't believe her ears, "What do you mean?" she asked, incredulous, "What's happened?"

The child detached herself enough for Daphne to see radiant pleasure in the little girl's features, "Everyone in school thinks I'm the luckiest person alive..." Cassandra giggled, "... because I live on a canal boat."

"But..." Daphne was bemused, "I don't understand..." She looked up, and saw James Erin smiling back at her from the jetty.

"I think I can explain," he said.

"Mummy," Cassandra whispered, "Mister Erin is my new teacher."

Daphne looked up at the man in front of her. He grinned, a little sheepishly, "I didn't realize until I got to the school," he said, "but Cassandra is in my class this year. I discovered there'd been some bullying, because she lived on a boat, so I made it clear that I lived on a boat too. That seemed to change their attitudes somewhat. Everyone envies her now."

"But, why did you bring her home?" Daphne asked, desperately trying to assimilate these latest developments.

"Two reasons, really," he replied, shifting a little nervously from one foot to the other, "To let the other kids know I consider Cassandra just as good as they are…though, of course in future she will get the school bus as normal, but…' he looked abashed, "…the other reason was really an excuse…"

"An excuse?" Daphne eyed him with curiosity.

He seemed unsure of himself, hesitant. "Yes," he said, "an excuse to see you…to…to ask if you would…perhaps, have dinner with me…help me celebrate my birthday tonight?"

Daphne still needed time to absorb these rapidly changing circumstances. In a moment, all she had feared was about to happen in her life had dissolved away. She was aware of Cassandra giggling, "Go on, Mummy…say yes. Auntie Jean from *'Ragdoll'* will baby-sit me."

"I…I…I'd love to," she stammered, feeling a great weight rising from her shoulders. Realization struck as a thunderbolt. Her mind, fogged by days of depression and indecision, suddenly was clear again. "Yes, I'd really love to have dinner with you tonight, James. Thank you…" then she added, "…but first, I've something I must do…straight away." She consulted her watch, "Yes, it's not too late."

After informing her dinner date she would meet him at seven-thirty, and bundling Cassandra into the cabin with instructions to change out of her new school uniform at once, Daphne marched purposefully down the pontoon and along the marina pathway, until she arrived at the door of the Sales Office. She opened it and went inside.

The lad was alone. He looked up as she entered, "Ah, I'm glad yer've called in," he began, "Mister an' Missus Blunt, them people what viewed yer boat this mornin', 'ave made an offer...it's a bit low, I'm afraid, but if yer wanna quick sale... I'd advise yer to accept it...in the circumstances..."

The offer was derisory. Daphne left, closing the door quietly behind her.

Inside, the beetroot-faced sales lad picked up a telephone to ring the Blunts. He would explain nicely that their offer was refused. But he would certainly refrain from telling them to shove it where Daphne Forbes-Jackson had suggested.

THE QUEEN OF DIXIE'S MARINA

It was one of those bitterly cold, wet and windy, New Year's Eve nights that Molly and I first met. I had just broken up with the current girlfriend and was not in the most festive of moods driving back to Dixie's Marina in the early hours. It had been a quarrel not easily forgotten. Well, certainly not until the bruise on my arm healed, from the ashtray she hurled across the kitchen, and her nail scratches on my cheek eventually ceased to sting like I'd used battery acid instead of shaving cream.

To top it all, I knew I wouldn't quite make the marina before a call of nature became too painful for further endurance, so with a muttered curse at the thought of vacating my warm cocoon on wheels, I braked sharply, steering the car to a halt alongside a farmer's field and a convenient gateway.

At that hour the country lane was pitch dark and totally deserted, or so I thought. Feeling huge relief, I turned back

117

towards the car when a faint and muffled, high-pitched cry caused me to hesitate. At first I thought it was just the trees creaking in the wind, but then I heard it again. The noise emanated from a drainage ditch alongside the lane. I grabbed a torch from the glove compartment and went searching. In the long grass at the bottom of the trench lay a black, plastic bag. It was moving, and a further muffled cry confirmed the contents to be alive and in need of assistance.

With no thought of the possible consequences I grabbed the bag, heaved it out of the ditch, and tore at the plastic. It ripped apart easily. The torchlight illumined one small, tabby kitten, no more than six weeks old. Dazzled and bewildered, it spat and hissed, ears flattened to a minuscule head. I reached down and grabbed at it with my free hand, whereupon needle-sharp fangs sank into my fingers, while simultaneously rear claws savagely raked the skin from the inside of my wrist.

Under attack for the second time that evening, I hurriedly stuffed the writhing, hissing, bundle into an old sports bag kept in the back of the car, zipped all but the last inch, and dabbing at the blood oozing from numerous tiny welts, I restarted the engine and drove the last mile to the marina.

My narrowboat was a warm and cosy refuge from the wild, winter night. I opened up the stove-flu and dabbed antiseptic on my wounds, before turning attention to the sports bag now resting on the saloon floor.

Carefully unzipping the top, observation of my furry antagonist revealed a more subdued creature, the bedraggled bundle scarcely hissing as I stroked its head with one finger.

After five minutes, it tolerated lifting onto the carpet and a saucer of warm milk. Within ten minutes, it was fast asleep on the rug in front of the saloon stove.

I poured myself a stiff drink and went to examine my face in the bathroom mirror.

"Thank you, Molly Armstrong...and a Happy New Year to you," I muttered dourly, gingerly massaging the three vivid red welts inflaming my left cheek, "I don't suppose I'll be seeing you again."

I returned to the saloon in time to witness my new acquaintance yawn vigorously and stretch two front paws full reach, before curling to a ball and retiring into dreamland once more.

While intent on the warm milk, I had taken the opportunity to lift a tail and ascertain the gender of this latest guest. I rubbed my wrist, still smarting from the kitten's claws, but couldn't resist a grin. "Two she-cats in one night...one out, one in. Looks like you've got yourself a name... Molly!"

The newcomer proved herself both intelligent and fiercely independent. She learnt her lessons quickly, and within a few weeks had settled into boat life like it was second nature.

Molly would meow to be let out first thing in the morning. Once the cabin door was open she would run up the steps, across the rear deck and leap dexterously over the narrow gap between boat and jetty. The narrowboat was moored close to the main canal, starboard side against the end jetty of a long pontoon. It was quite a way up the wooden slats to the marina carpark, to grassy areas suitable for her needs, but it was not long before Molly considered herself the Queen of Dixie's Marina, and moved around the grounds with confidence, though always alert to possible danger.

She was so confident, that soon the journey from cabin to jetty would be completed in three or four bounds. Once on the wooden slats, she would sit a moment and look around, then a quick lick of a wash and up the pontoon to complete her toilet.

One afternoon, about a month after Molly came to stay, the water tank ran dry and I cruised down to the faucet in front of 'Betty's Canal Emporium'. It was only fifty yards, and usually after filling the tank I reversed back onto the mooring, but on this occasion I fancied a change of view from the galley window and turned the boat around, mooring portside to the jetty.

Next morning while cooking breakfast, I let Molly out as usual. It was an early spring day, warm enough to leave the cabin door open. I settled back to enjoy bacon and eggs, when from the corner of my vision something moved on the stern fender. First a paw, then a bedraggled head appeared, closely followed by the rest of a soaking wet and very unhappy kitten.

Molly had bounded up the steps as usual, across the deck and over the side before the realization dawned that the jetty was no longer there. I never heard the splash, but she must have swum around to the stern, grabbed at the rope fender with a claw and heaved herself back onboard. I wrapped the unfortunate creature in a towel and took her below to dry off.

Molly continued to live on my narrowboat for a further seven years, but never once crossed the back deck again without first stopping halfway, to check which side of the boat was against the jetty. It was a hard lesson, but one she always remembered.

As spring turned to summer, Molly matured into a fine looking animal. She always remained fiercely independent and her intelligence amazed me. I had kept cats before, but none like Molly. In many ways she was more like a dog, and would follow at my heels whenever I left the boat to begin the day's work. When I entered the office, she would 'meow' goodbye and go about her own business, whatever that might be. By five-thirty, I would find her waiting patiently at the entrance to the pontoon, ready to follow at my heels as I returned to the boat for the evening. Where Molly went through the day remained a mystery, but the farmer's fields around the marina were a hunter's paradise, and often on returning to the boat I would find a dead mouse or vole obligingly left for me outside the cabin door.

Molly loved boats, but hated engines. The first job of the evening, after removing any dead rodents from the doorstep, was to fire up the big diesel beneath the sterndeck and charge the batteries. Immediately on sensing the vibrations, Molly would take to her heels and disappear up the pontoon. Later, usually just minutes after I had shut the engine down, she would wander back into the cabin unperturbed and settle down for the night.

This created a problem whenever I contemplated a few days cruising on the canal. I would have to shut Molly in the cabin until we were far enough from the bank for her not to jump off the boat. She sulked abominably, and when I let her out on deck would slink around, behaving badly, until a narrow bridge-hole allowed her to leap onto the towpath. There, she would sit and meow piteously as the boat pulled away, as though denouncing me for deliberately abandoning her.

I became expert at reversing back into bridge-holes, but determined to persevere until Molly finally accepted the vagaries of the diesel engine. Needless to say, she never did. Eventually, I realised her sensitive survival instincts were swamped by such noisy vibrations, and came to understand and accept the insecurity this generated within her.

She, in turn, did her best to acknowledge that there were times she had no choice but to be onboard. On long trips I would lift her onto the cabin roof, from where she was loathe to leap off, even at bridge-holes, and would eventually curl up and sleep most of the time, albeit begrudgingly.

Molly only made two visits to the veterinary clinic in all the years we were together; once as a kitten for vaccinations, and a few months later for the dread 'operation'. Neither appeared to cause her serious trauma. The seven days I had determined she would remain indoors for the stitches to do their work, shrank to two when Molly decided she would definitely not use a litter tray, when the whole outside world was for her convenience. Apart from an occasional lick at the wound during regular toilet, she disdained to admit anything wrong with her abdomen, and continued life as usual once, after a sleepless night spent listening to her plaintive cries, I relented and let her out.

Canines soon learned to give Molly a wide berth. A number of moorers brought their dogs to the marina and they soon realised she was not the usual domestic feline, to be barked at and chased like a rabbit. It was rare for any dog to venture near Molly. They seemed to recognize the aura of authority emanating from the Queen of Dixie's Marina and would move rapidly in another direction, or tuck themselves close under their owner's heels, whenever she appeared in their path.

Sometimes, when the mood took her, Molly would slink behind a gatepost or moored boat, then leap out, back arched, ears flattened, on some unfortunate canine passing innocently by. This behaviour usually resulted in a thoroughly demoralized dog high-tailing back in the direction of its owner's boat. Mostly, she majestically ignored them all, with the noticeable exception of Joey.

Joey was best described as a 'crossbred something crossed with a crossbred something'. He was a small, wire-haired terrier with a tan coat heavily impregnated by the grey of maturity. Joey was old and a bit arthritic and spent most summer weekends sleeping on the back deck of his owner's fibreglass cruiser, *'Maggie May'*.

One Saturday morning, I was strolling up the pontoon on my way to the office, with Mollie at my heels, when a cacophony of barking and growling erupted in the car park. Joey lay cowed on the gravel surrounded by several other dogs, all obviously ganging up on him and spoiling for a fight. Joey was no match for one, let alone several. I was just on the point of going in and chasing them when Molly left my side, squeezed deftly under the fence, and stalked purposefully towards the group. The dogs saw her approach, stopped tormenting the unfortunate Joey and looked hesitantly, first at her, then at each other. Molly stopped about ten feet from the group, and just stared. The dogs' tails, pert at the prospect of mischief, began to sag. One by one they backed away from the prostrate terrier. Then the ringleader, a young German Shepherd from *'Hunter's Moon'*, turned and sauntered casually off up the marina, and the others quickly followed suit.

Joey raised himself to a sitting position as Molly strolled over. The two touched noses and the cat lifted a front paw, lightly tapping the old dog on his cheek. Then, side by side, they walked casually off up the marina in the direction of *'Maggie May'*.

It was the beginning of an amazing friendship. From then on, Joey and Molly would often be seen walking together around the marina. Molly usually took the lead and the old dog, stiff-legged, followed obligingly behind. Sometimes they could be seen asleep, curled up together on the back deck of *'Maggie May'* or in the long grass that bordered the margin of George Anderson's farmland.

Molly always knew instinctively when Joey was at the marina. Through the week, she never went looking for him, or acknowledged in any way that he ever existed, and yet Eric Mathieson, Joey's owner, often related how Mollie would appear outside his boat within five or ten minutes of their arrival at the marina. It became something of a standing joke. Each weekend, he would point knowingly at his wristwatch, "Only eight minutes this week," he would say with a grin, or, "Took her quart o' an hour this morning. Joey were gettin' quite worried...thought she'd found another suitor."

And so it went on. Joey was never again bothered by other dogs so long as the Queen of Dixie's Marina was his friend, which she always was right up till the day, some two years after they first met, that Joey stopped coming with Eric and his wife to spend the weekend on *'Maggie May'*. Arthritis turned to bone cancer and the veterinarian shook his head and reached for his hypodermic needle.

As for Molly, she never gave any indication of missing Joey and continued to rule her domain for another five years, until I sold my narrowboat and moved to a cottage in the countryside. Molly came with me and settled as easily to life ashore, as she had afloat. Two years on, I retired and circumstances took me to live in America. Much as I would have wished Molly with me, she was getting old and spent most days sleeping contentedly in the sunshine, on the banks of a stream that gurgled past the cottage. The new owners loved her on sight and were very happy to make her part of the fixtures and fittings. So, with heavy heart, I flew off to a new life in America leaving the Queen of Dixie's Marina to her retirement. I never saw her again, but just occasionally I'll dig out an old photograph, or the tattered yellow collar I took from her as a keepsake, and I'll remember that wild and windy New Year's Eve night when one Molly walked out of my life forever, and another moved in.

Printed in the United Kingdom
by Lightning Source UK Ltd.
130883UK00001B/64/P